How to Lose Control in 42 Days

An Age-Gap Novella

Brookelyn Mosley

85 Media

More By Brookelyn Mosley

Links to the below stories can be found here (https://brookelynmosley.com/ebooks-paperbacks/)

Novels/Novellas/Novelettes/Series

- No Fraternizing, Pt. 1
- No Fraternizing, Pt. 2
- No Fraternizing, Pt. 3
- First Came Love: The Love, Hate & Revenge Prequel
- Love, Hate & Revenge, Pt. 1
- Love, Hate & Revenge, Pt. 2
- Love, Hate & Revenge, Pt. 3
- Girl Code
- Mr. & Mrs. Jones
- Forbidden: An Anthology
- They Call Me Mello
- A Love Deferred
- Indecent Arrangement
- Last Comes Love
- Ebb & Flow
- PRIDE
- Meant To Be
- LUST
- Loveless
- GREED
- Rekindled

• My First, My Last

• ENVY

• Ready or Not

• So This is Love

• Home Before Midnight

• GLUTTONY

• When Luke Met Juliette

• When Life Gives You Sunsets

• In Love, I Trust

• Wrath

• Sloth

• Raising Love

• My Only

Short Stories

• Unsilent Knight

• Twice In Love

• Home For Christmas

BYBK EXCLUSIVES

Bed Bully
Stuck
LHR Rewind Series
Home Before Midnight
Maybe This Time Will Be Different
Lovekilla
Incoming Call
Rough
WYD
Drinks on Me
Cali & Lee
Ray & Jay
Living Out a Love Song
Glimpses
One Mic
With Love, Ayanna & Dallas
Just Friends
Lena's Ex-File
Dream Boss
Chateau Luxure

Second Serving
Glimpses Vol. 2

Acknowledgments

As always, I want to thank my husband first and foremost. I do so in every book because it's through our conversations that some of my favorite story ideas are born. You've been my biggest fan from the very start—even when I was unsure of myself—and I'm grateful to you for seeing me before I ever could. Thank you.

To my children, who keep me on my toes and help me balance real life with fiction... you're demanding, and Mommy loves that about you. Always stay the same. I appreciate you more than you know.

To my readers—you're always on my mind as I write. I know when you'll love a character and when you'll hate them, because I usually feel those emotions first. Thank you for allowing me to get to know you and, through you, to learn so much about myself. Thank you for trusting my pen, always.

And finally, I want to thank myself. It's a new acknowledgment, but one I'm learning to honor, to give love to myself the way I give it to others. These have been turbulent times, and still, I show up and give my best. That takes courage, determination, and discipline I once didn't believe I had. I'm thankful I keep showing up... and for how often I manage to blow my own damn mind!

Message from the Author

Thank you for purchasing *How to Lose Control in 42 Days*.

This story is a novella and features new characters in my book world. Though Arielle was briefly mentioned in *My Only*, her story truly begins here. So if you're new to my writing, this is a great place to start your journey.

A quick note before you begin:

This story explores themes of grief and captures the transition of a parent. If that's something you may find difficult to read, please take care of yourself and read when you're ready.

Thank you for embarking on Arielle and Micah's love journey. This story is the first of its kind for me—one that explores surrender, healing, and rediscovering joy—and I hope you love reading it as much as I loved writing it.

Enjoy.

With love,

BK

To Teri Joseph, whose story in Soul Food inspired this one... and to the daughters who inherit not just a family name, but the unseen burdens that come with it. This is for you...

Day 1: Lose Your Cool

ARIELLE

The ding of the elevator as it glided down floors sounded around me.

"I know there's a brain in there," I said into the phone, switching my device from one ear to the other. "Let's be responsible and use it, Julian."

"Don't start with me, Ari," he voiced. "Not today."

"So what day would be best to discuss a $25K mistake?" The elevator dinged once more. "This afternoon? Next week? Oh, I know... never, right?"

"It was a business expense."

"No, Julian," I said through my teeth, just as the chrome doors split open in front of me. "A Birkin is *not* a business expense."

"Karmen was photo'd in it, and it made *Page Six*."

I gritted my teeth as my heels clicked against the polished floors of my building.

"The Birkin is a part of our brand's image, isn't it?"

"Thank you," I said to my doorman as he held the door open for me.

The mild mid-spring air brushing against my face was exactly what I needed to keep my cool.

"Karmen is intentionally assisting with our brand's visibility," Julian continued on the other end of my phone. "You have to admit... it's clever marketing, Ari."

I forced a smile at valet as I made my way to the driver's side door of my S-Class.

"Good morning, Ms. St. James." The valet attendant smiled as he held my car door open for me.

"Good morning," I offered, sliding into the seat. "Thank you. Have a good one."

As soon as the attendant shut my door and I sank into the smooth leather, my phone beeped with another call before I could even get comfortable.

I moved my phone off my ear for only a moment to see that it was my brother calling.

"Look," I said to Julian as I placed my bag on the passenger seat. "I'm just leaving my penthouse and heading to the hotel now. We're going to finish this in a meeting."

"A meeting?!" Julian shrieked. "For what?"

"To discuss you buying a fucking Birkin for your wife with your company credit card, Julian. Are you kidding me?"

"Operative word here, Ari," he countered. "*My* card."

My phone beeped again.

"I have to go."

"We're not married anymore, or did you forget? Your choice, remember? So with that said, you don't get to police my expenses."

I rolled my eyes. "Get off my phone, Julian."

I ended the call, switched to the next line, and set the phone on speaker.

My hand was reaching for my seatbelt, eyes scanning the area in front of me as I secured the buckle when my brother started speaking before I could greet him.

"Your father is at it again, Ari."

I sighed, leaning forward over the wheel to ease out of my parking spot.

"Good morning, Miles," I said, projecting just enough for the speaker. "How are you?"

"*We're* not good," my other brother, the youngest, Langston, said next.

"Oh joy. Three-way." I rolled my tongue around my mouth, a habit, my eyes scanning the city streets through my windshield. "How did you two know *that's* what I wanted to deal with this morning?"

They both sighed exaggeratedly into the phone.

I stopped at the red light and leaned my head back against my headrest, rolling it from left to right, allowing my eyes to close for only a moment.

First, I had to deal with my ex-husband trying to justify charging $25K on our company card to buy his new wife a bag, and now this.

Typical Arielle St. James morning, unfortunately.

"Let's hear it," I told them, lifting my head just as the light turned green. "Where's the fire today?"

"In your father's brain," Miles started. "He's lost his mind, again."

Miles was the middle of us three, the ladies' man with a résumé full of almosts. He'd tried his hand at everything except the hotel business... which was how our empire stayed an empire.

For the past two years, he'd been working in wine importing. The year before, he was running a trendy boutique in SoHo before he got bored with that.

Our dad loved him the very most. Probably because Miles never told Dad how he felt about him and his decisions. Miles would only tell me... and convince me to go and talk to Dad about it.

One of the perks of being the eldest.

That was sarcasm, by the way.

"He told us he just signed a letter of intent to open a Black luxury fishing resort in Montauk," Langston said next. "Of all places. Said that part of Long Island could use some color."

Langston was the youngest and the one who *hated* being a St. James as much as he loved it. Hated it because of our father. Loved it because of our name's prestige, and the money that came with it.

"Dad said it's Black Nantucket meets Wakanda," Miles started again. "I don't even know what that means."

I was approaching traffic when I shook my head — at my brothers, at traffic, at the whole damn morning.

I should've taken a damn cab.

"So..." I said, tightening my grip around the steering wheel. "What did he say when you two approached him about it? How did he justify his vision, his plan? Did he share his plans with either of you—"

"Technically, I haven't spoken to him about it, *per se*," Miles said first. "I'm in Italy. He called me while I was visiting a vineyard. I *lied*. Told him it was a great idea but it's horrible, right?"

I rolled my eyes. "And how about you, Langston?"

"I'm in Iceland. On sabbatical. I wasn't about to deal with that."

I blinked hard. "Sabbatical?"

"I needed the reprieve for my mental health, clearly," he reasoned. "The city can be taxing on me and I often need to get out. You know that. And thank *God* I'm not there, because *look* what he's doing now."

"Let me make sure I understand what's happening here," I said, turning onto a new city block. I was only a few blocks away from my hotel. "You two are out of the country but complaining about Dad doing something you don't like, and you're not even here for us all to have a sit-down about it?"

"We were hoping *you* could do it," Langston said. "You know... like always."

"Like always," I repeated flatly.

"Dad listens to you," Miles tried. Well... more like lied. "Plus, you're the best at handling stuff like this. You have a better way with words than Langston and me."

Translation: I'm the sibling that's easier to hate — because our father already resented me for being the firstborn and female... not that he'd ever admit it.

And, no. *That*? Was *not* sarcasm.

The red light I stopped at switched to green, and before I could even lift my foot off the brakes, a black Range Rover sped up in front of me, cutting me off.

I gasped. "Motherfu—"

I swallowed the rest of my words and instead inhaled a deep breath to remain cool.

"So do you think you can do it today, Ari?" Miles asked, bringing me back into the conversation. "It would be ideal to snip this in the bud as soon as possible."

"Fine," I replied, reluctantly. "Don't I always handle the dirty work?"

"That's what big sisters are for, right?" Langston chimed in next.

I shook my head as I approached another red light.

Our dad, Harold St. James, called himself retired, but that was just in theory. In reality, he was still very attached to the family empire I managed with my brothers. But he hadn't contributed meaningfully in years... much like my brothers.

The light switched to green again, and just like a few blocks behind me, the same black Range sped up in front, cutting me off once more.

"What the hell is this person's problem?" I gritted behind my teeth.

"Ari?" Langston asked. "Are you still there?"

I stared at the red taillights as they moved further and further away. A breath later, I stepped on the gas a little harder than usual to close the distance between me and them.

"I'll handle it," I said, eyes locked in on the black Range Rover. "I'm heading into the hotel. I'll call you two later."

Before they could give me a response, I ended the call... just in time to maneuver my car up beside the black Range Rover at the next red light.

The windows were already down in the truck when I pulled up beside it on the passenger side.

I was seconds away from unloading on him for cutting me off at not one, but two green lights when my words got caught in my throat.

He was handsome. *Very* handsome. And young. Not who I was expecting to see behind the wheel of a truck like this... and also not expecting him to be so unbothered.

He peeked over at me, locking eyes through the lowered passenger window... holding my attention like he meant to. Low-lidded eyes. Clear brown skin that looked soft even at a distance. A manicured beard framed thick, two-toned lips that parted just enough—like he was on the verge of saying something slick. Then, with maddening calm, he gave me a simple head nod. A wordless hello.

"Oh, hey there," I quipped. "Do you mind not cutting me off?"

He blinked in response.

"You did it twice back there," I noted. "It's very rude."

"My fault. I apologize."

Those four little words came out of his mouth wrapped in a smooth, warm texture. Also *not* what I was expecting from someone who drove like a maniac.

"I can't do anything with an apology for something that's already happened."

"Oh, nah, my bad." He smiled. "I'm apologizing in advance. 'Cause I plan to cut you off again. Sorry."

As soon as the light turned green, he sure enough did it again.

Cutting into my lane beneath the light and speeding down the block.

At that point, my jaw was dropped, pulse racing. I couldn't decide if I was pissed that he'd cut me off again... or intrigued by how good he looked doing it.

"What an asshole," I mumbled to myself.

I definitely should have taken a cab to work.

I was in front of *The St. James* in short time, my valet there to open my door and greet me.

I made my way to the front doors of *The St. James* and inhaled a valiant deep breath to brace myself.

As stunningly beautiful as it was—with its five-star-rated restaurant, *The St. James Table*; the much-talked-about rooftop bar and lounge, *Vesper*; and the 40 thoughtfully appointed rooms —*The St. James* was a staple in Manhattan in all its Black-owned luxury glory.

Known for its intimate hospitality experience, *The St. James* was the standard for discerning guests who valued discretion, taste, and status.

We'd won awards for our impeccable service and quiet sophistication, most of which curated by me.

This location in New York was the first joint business between myself and my ex-husband, Julian... until he ruined everything by having an affair with his now wife.

"Good morning, Ms. St. James," my assistant Charmaine greeted the second I stepped through my office door.

"Good morning, Charm," I said, dropping my bag onto my gold-rimmed glass desk and plopping into my leather chair. "I need coffee. Immediately. Large. Very, *very* black. Nothing in it— not even sweetener. I need all the damn caffeine this morning, actually, with *no* interference *or* interruptions—"

"Oh! *Umm... damn.*" She bit her bottom lip nervously. "You've got that bartender interview today... remember?"

"Excuse me?"

"Rooftop. Five minutes." She gestured to the ceiling with her pen. "It's been in your calendar all week."

"Wait, I thought Julian was handling that," I stated. "Wasn't it in *his* calendar? I was just cc'd on as a courtesy."

"He said he's booked," she said, her voice small. "Said *you* can handle it."

"Of course he said that." I closed my eyes for a second, then took a deep breath to keep it together. "How much time do I have before the bartender arrives?"

"They're already here," she replied. "And waiting behind *Vesper's* bar."

"Perfect," I forced out. "Just perfect."

I wish I could say this was a surprise—Julian dropping yet another thing in my lap that he was supposed to handle—but that would be a lie. This was par for the course. So there was no use dwelling on his incompetence now.

The St. James brand ran on the perception of order. I couldn't have even an applicant waiting because someone else didn't handle what they were supposed to.

Some days, though, I wanted to drop it all. Walk away without a worry or a care. *Dare to dream.* I'd fantasize about what that freedom might taste like... mornings with no meetings, no board calls, no one needing me to fix their mistakes.

But then reality would creep back in. Everything would fall apart without me. And I'd invested *too much* to let that happen.

I ran my fingers through my silk-pressed natural hair, smoothed a hand down my blazer, then over my dress pants before pushing my chair back to stand.

"Well, all right." I rolled back my shoulders, fighting back fatigue. "Let's get to it."

I stalked toward my office door, only turning back for the clipboard Charmaine walked in with.

"Is this their résumé?"

"It is," she said, handing it over. "Very impressive. Worked at The Four Seasons at their in-house bar last. Has a good amount of experience working their kitchen. They also have serving experience."

"Jack of all trades, huh?" I mumbled, already irritated. "Master of none, I'm sure."

This was the fourth bartender I was interviewing within six months. They just didn't seem to last long here. *The St. James*, as popular as it was, had a huge turnover when it came to service people.

They were all simply in the city hustling, using their time at *The St. James* to supplement their incomes until they got their big break.

I understood this when I decided to open this hotel with Julian.

My family-owned multiple hotels around the globe — from Aspen to South Beach — with a boutique property in London.

But *The St. James* in New York was the crown jewel of all the properties, even if it were the newest addition.

I listened to Charmaine rattle off all of the things I'd already read on the bartender's résumé on our way up to *Vesper*, our skyline bar and lounge.

I never could appreciate how beautiful Manhattan looked from up here. Because I was too busy stressing about the stuff I was dealing with on the ground.

"Thanks, Charm," I said to her. "I'll take it from here."

My eyes were down on the clipboard, reading through the résumé items.

Having walked these floors so many mornings, noons, and nights, I blindly pushed open the glass door that led to the rooftop bar and stepped in.

My eyes were still skimming through the résumé as I approached.

I lifted my head... just long enough to see the guy from the black Range Rover standing behind our bar's glass counter.

His presence made me lose my footing for only a moment, but I quickly regained control.

He dropped his head back in reaction to seeing me and released a breathy laugh, leveled his gaze again to reveal a very handsome smile.

"Small world, huh?" he commented.

I slammed the clipboard onto the bar's glass counter.

Peeked down at the name on the résumé.

A name I'd paid little attention to... until I saw who was attached to it.

Micah Black.

"I didn't want to be late," he started, pulling my attention back to him. "I wasn't trying to cut you off just to be a dick. You were just driving way too slow."

I arched a brow.

"From my view, you were on a call, you seemed distracted, so..." He folded his arms over his broad chest and shrugged. "I moved around you."

"Rudely," I finally said.

"Safely," he said. "Efficiently. Is what I'd say."

"How old are you?"

The question was more out of curiosity than relevance.

"Twenty-eight years young."

Hard blink.

I blinked a little too quickly. Hopefully he didn't notice.

How was he *only* twenty-eight years old?

He looked way too casual-cool, too out of place to be this confident... and to be twenty-eight.

With communicative eyes and a knowing grin that made me feel like we could check the same age box.

"And you?"

I jerked my head back. "Excuse me?"

"How old are *you*?"

I laughed. "None of your business."

He grinned. "You asked me about my age."

"Because *you* want to work for *me*. I need to make sure you're legal."

"*Mmm-hmm.*" He licked his lips. "Aight. You got that."

We held our stares for a moment, my heart doing something familiar at the wrong possible time.

I snatched my eyes off him when I realized I'd been staring for too long.

Focused on the glass bar counter, then at the drinks lining the glass shelves behind him.

Everywhere but at him... for valid reasons.

I refocused on him and said, "I perused your résumé. Impressive. You have more experience than your age should allow."

He nodded.

I lowered my eyes to his resume again, to scan his work history. "You've worked in a lot of places, Micah."

"Yeah." He cleared his throat, regaining my focus. "I've had to move around a bit. Family stuff. Timing never lined up the way I wanted it to so I did what I could with what I had. Been working since I was thirteen, so... yeah."

I squinted my eyes at that. *Moved around a lot. Timing never lining up.* All things that made me curious. Not as much as *when* he started working. At thirteen. He was thirteen only fifteen years ago... and I was twenty-five.

I don't even know why my brain did that math.

"Make me a drink," I blurted, hoping to shift the moment. Shift myself? "Imagine I'm a St. James patron who has approached the bar in search of something, but I don't know what I want. Make me something you think I'd like."

He arched both brows.

"Because that's part of what we do here, and one of the reasons our last bartender, who worked the shift you're interviewing for, quit after three days. And the other, after a week," I explained. "Guests don't just stay here. They belong. It's a home away from home, and at home, everything is familiar. Something our last few bartenders couldn't quite grasp. So I want to try something different with you. Make me something familiar."

"Isn't it too early for a drink?"

"It's cocktail hour somewhere on the globe, right?"

And God, I needed something after all the stuff I've had to manage before noon.

A smile slowly pulled at the corners of his lips as he maintained eye contact with me.

"How about *you* make it?"

I tilted my head to one side.

"I'll instruct you."

"For someone with *so much* experience," I started, "I would think you'd know how an interview works. In case you're forgetting, you're going to be working for me."

"And to prove how amazing *I* am at what *I* do, I'm going to instruct *you*..." He pointed. "To make a drink."

I blinked twice.

"You said it yourself." He pressed his big hands onto the glass counter. "Y'all have been blowing through bartenders left and right because they're not getting it. You want to try something new with me? Let's *really* try something new. I'm sure you've never mixed a drink in your life, and if I can teach you to do it, imagine what I can do when I'm behind your bar... actually working it alone."

I looked off, considering his words.

"I could mix one drink and it be great for sure," he continued. "But I'm sure you want the confidence of someone experienced enough to run your bar with the standards that make *The St. James* a place to belong. So, let's do it."

He rubbed his hands together as he stepped back from the bar, his eyes moving all over it before reaching for this and that: a bottle of mezcal, a silver shaker, orange bitters.

Those were a few of the things that made it onto the counter.

He asked, "Are you ready?"

I didn't know why I didn't hesitate to step closer instead of asked him to leave.

Maybe it was his tone.

Maybe it was the fact that no one ever dared to instruct *me*.

Someone ordering me to do something was foreign, honestly... but intriguing too.

Who was this kid?

"Ice in the shaker," he said. "Not too much. Just enough to wake it up and not drown it."

I did as told, following the rest of his instructions to a T.

I poured the mezcal and elderflower liqueur. Actually squeezed the lime juice, feeling as it dripped down my fingers, because Micah swore that the bottled lime juice wouldn't do.

Lifted the ginger syrup in curiosity.

"Because I can tell you like spice," he said.

"I don't," I lied.

He snickered. "*Mmm-hmm.*"

Two dashes of bitters and a stir—not a shake—because as he put it...

"This isn't chaos. It's control."

I strained the drink in a coupe and flamed an orange peel last, because he swore it would make a difference.

And when I stepped back, I was impressed with what the drink looked like.

It looked phenomenal.

"Now take a sip." He grinned, cockily. "Tell me I'm wrong... or tell me if I nailed what I strongly believed you'd like."

And when I did, I was stunned.

Shocked.

Absolutely pleased—not only with the fact that he'd had me make a drink that was so me...

He had me make a damn drink. Period.

"Fuck," I said, a little too loudly.

I heard a short laugh escape him and immediately snapped my eyes over to him, the taste lingering on my tongue.

I swallowed hard next, then dropped my eyes to the glass, a little embarrassed I'd lost my cool, tasting such an incredible drink.

The spice offered the kind of bite I never knew I needed.

I would've never thought to mix any of this stuff together.

Would've never thought it would make *this*.

I stared at the glass, for a moment longer forgetting where I was.

For the first time in a long time, I felt... light. Weightless. All from making a damn drink myself.

I couldn't help the smile that pulled at my lips.

I came up here to screen a candidate to run my bar. This was an interview, not a date. I had to be in charge. Control was my thing, my armor, my guarantee. But somehow, with one drink, he'd loosened my grip.

I lifted my eyes to his, to see his fixed attention on me.

Blinked then quickly cleared my throat and ran my hand down my hair.

"That was... different."

He grinned. "Impeccable?"

Unforgettable.

"I said what I said," I voiced instead. "Different."

Humor etched his face.

"The position is yours," I told him with a nod.

"Shifts alternate weekly, so you won't work the same afternoons and nights, but we're flexible—we'll work with your availability. But hey..." I held a finger up. "If I see any of that reckless behavior you demonstrated earlier on your way here? You're gone. I don't give warnings, Micah. I just fire people... with a smile. Do you understand?"

He nodded, not at all threatened by anything I'd said.

"Yes, ma'am," he added with a smile of his own.

That smile. That voice.

I hated how it warmed my skin just hearing it.

I wasn't all that sure about Micah, but being sure didn't matter.

I needed a bartender—and he seemed to be a great one—and that would have to do.

I couldn't ignore that *thing* my heart did every time he smiled at me, though.

But I would have to.

Because I wasn't going to make the same mistake twice with a man.

Look where it got me with Julian—stuck in a business partnership where I was balancing both our responsibilities, all while arguing with him about charging an expensive bag for the mistress he married to spite me for divorcing him.

Yeah, there was *no way* I was falling for that trap again.

And Micah was practically a child? No thank you.

But damn, I couldn't lie to myself even if I wanted to...

He would definitely be something to look forward to seeing at *The St. James*.

DAY 3: LOSE YOUR LABEL

MICAH

I bobbed my head in time with the soft rhythm of the saxophone.

Jazz played around me, low, and in competition with the hum of the oxygen tank.

My eyes were fixed on my dad, Leonard, who was asleep, on his in-home hospital bed.

I inhaled the air, picking up traces of the lavender I'd rubbed on his temples an hour prior, and the antiseptic from the medicinal solutions lingering beneath the essential oil.

Settling more into the armchair, I stretched my legs out and my arms high above my head, then dropped my head back.

My eyes burned a little, but that was aight.

It was aight for now... because I was here for my dad who has always been there for me. Plus, I knew how to escape mentally.

Some nights, in the hum of that oxygen tank, I'd drift. Think about starting fresh somewhere else... France, maybe. I've always wanted to go. But that was just a fantasy. A thought I'd never say out loud.

I lifted my wrist to check the time as soon as I heard the key turn in the door's lock down the hall.

It was time for me to head out.

"Hey," Ms. Thea greeted behind me, entering the bedroom. "Good morning."

I turned in my seat to face her. "Good morning, Ms. Thea."

She smiled, her eyes moving to my sleeping father. "How was he last night?"

I nodded slowly, inhaling a breath as I sat up in my seat. "He was aight. Still here and hanging in there."

"Nine months past the doctor's estimate." Ms. Thea giggled, setting her bag on the table beside my dad's hospital bed. "A stubborn heart, in every sense."

I chuckled.

She ran her hand over his forehead, then pressed her hand to his chest. Sighed, then looked to me.

"You better get going." She lifted her wrist to check her watch. "Don't you have to be in Tribeca in an hour?"

I nodded.

"Then go 'head." She gestured to the door with her chin. "Before you're late."

"Oh, I'm never late. You know me." I winked. "I'll be there in half an hour, maybe sooner than that."

She suppressed a laugh, then wagged a finger at me. "You better stop flying through these people's streets in that truck of yours, Mic."

I smiled this time, my attention moving over to my dad, feeling the lump form in my throat.

"You look like you lost a fight with your dreams last night."

I scoffed. "Didn't sleep long enough to have any."

Ms. Thea approached, laying a hand on my head and leaning it against her waist.

"It's good that you're working again."

"*Hmph,*" I huffed, my eyes returning to my father.

"Something to do, because you can't sit here waiting on death, Mic," she added. "You know your father wouldn't want that."

I nodded, not saying a word, because she was right.

"I just... don't want to miss anything. Or be too late. Or... whatever."

Her hold on my head tightened just a bit, and her comfort immediately sent an ache to my chest.

"I'll call you the moment there is any change," she promised. "*Any* change whatsoever, I'll call you."

"Aight." I nodded again. "Bet."

I sniffed back the tears that wanted to fall and pulled away long enough to stand to my feet.

"I rubbed lavender oil on his temples." I gestured at the tray of amber glass bottles with droppers lined neatly in a row. "Gave him his medicine and changed his bedpan."

She smiled. "And now he's all mine." She focused over at him. "Ain't that right, Lenny?"

The faint hum of his hospital bed was his only answer.

After freshening up, I was out of my hood in Crown Heights and heading toward posh-ass Tribeca.

I drove down black roads and between wide pedestrian walkways. Limestone row houses and pre-war buildings—like the one my dad and I have called home for over a decade—stood to my left and right. Caribbean flags waved from apartment windows and porches. Between the street art and murals were older signs and storefronts, blending in with newer, boutique-style spots.

I watched the world change outside my window. Watched it shift from my hood to something fancy.

A daily occurrence I didn't care to see. I really didn't want to leave my father's side.

But Ms. Thea was right.

Deciding to pick up bartending again instead of sitting by my father's bedside all day, waiting for him to take his last breath, was probably the wisest thing to do.

Ever since he got his prognosis last year—late-stage congestive heart failure, with the doctor telling us he only had three months to live—I'd dropped everything.

When the doctor said we should check him into hospice, my father refused. He wanted to die in the home he knew.

So, I quit my bartending job at an upscale lounge in SoHo and turned his bedroom into a home-hospice setup in a weekend. It wasn't even a decision. Just something that had to be done.

I didn't think about it. I just did it.

I told Ms. Thea my plans, and she offered to help make my father's final days comfortable.

She was a retired hospice nurse and my father's ex-girlfriend of seven years.

They didn't work out—my father never really got over losing my mom when I was fourteen—but they stayed friends. Thankfully.

Because if it wasn't for Ms. Thea, I have no idea how I would have made it this far.

I arrived at *The St. James* in under an hour, despite traffic... like I knew I would.

Day three behind the rooftop bar.

Still wild to think the woman I cut off in traffic was Arielle St. James, heiress to a hospitality empire.

Her dad, Harold St. James, was Black royalty, very well known. More for what he had than what he actually did.

Arielle though? She was known more by name than face. Which is why I didn't recognize her when I cut her off in traffic. All I knew then was she was gorgeous—long before I knew who she really was.

When I showed up for that interview, my only goal was to stand out enough to land the job. But the second she walked in, everything shifted. Standing out wasn't about the gig anymore... it was about *her*. About making sure, long after the interview ended, Arielle St. James remembered me. That's why I suggested she make the drink instead of me. I wanted her hands on the shaker, her lips on the glass, her eyes on me… and no chance of forgetting the bartender who dared flip the script.

And from that moment on, leaving Crown Heights for Tribeca was easy. Because ever since that interview, I wasn't just showing up to *The St. James* for the job. I was showing up for her.

I parked and walked into luxury.

A huge contrast from what I knew, but none of this was new to me.

I've worked in five-star restaurants, swanky bars and lounges.

It's been how I made my money for the past ten years—seven of those years spent bartending.

But *The St. James* was different…

Because it had *the* Arielle St. James.

On my way to my post at the bar upstairs, I purposely passed by her office door.

Behaving like a little boy with a crush, I know.

But damn, if there was anyone I could crush on, I was happy it was her.

"Good afternoon," I said, stopping at her office's doorway.

She was typing on her laptop when she moved her head in my direction, then pulled her eyes off the screen to focus on me. Her gaze scanned me from my black button-down, to the sleeves rolled up, stopping at my clean sneakers before moving her attention back up to meet mine again.

She was so damn crisp.

So composed.

And so fucking sexy, my God.

A beauty to rival the fine ass Lela Rochon in *Waiting to Exhale*. The film was one of my father's favorites—mostly because he liked watching the women in all their beauty on screen.

"Good afternoon." She held a stare with me. "Do you need something?"

I made a shrugging motion with the corners of my lips. "Nothing at all."

She blinked in response.

I flashed a smile and, just like the other times I flashed it, her shoulders lost a little height, and she took in a breath she didn't let go of.

"Just passing through. Couldn't start the day without saying... good afternoon."

It was subtle, but I noticed the beginnings of a smile.

She was so in control, she balled her lips and suppressed it, though.

The Arielle St. James.

A name that had appeared in Forbes.

The owner of a hotel brand people had been name-dropping in hip-hop songs and Black films lately.

Arielle was beyond a stunner.

She was pure light.

A high beam that walked like she owned the building... because she did.

And although her prestige would likely be the most attractive thing about her to the people around her, it was what she held back that intrigued me.

There was something in her eyes that looked like tired joy.

Something private. A secret.

And I loved uncovering secrets.

I liked the idea of uncovering her.

"Well, I won't hold you." I offered a simple nod. "Have a good rest of your day."

The rest of the afternoon moved swiftly.

I'd only been there for three days, but already, I noticed familiar faces that made their way to the rooftop lounge, *Vesper*—most notably the bar.

Most ordered boring drinks.

The women: fruity martinis.

The men: Scotches, brandy, some whiskeys. All neat.

The monotony was what I needed, though.

A nice temporary distraction. Predictability.

Everything was all good until the end of my shift.

Once the other bartender arrived and I collected my things to head out, the smooth, calm feel of the evening was disrupted the moment I made my way to the main floor of the hotel.

"Chef André is out sick," I heard murmured in a huddle of hotel staff I passed on my way to the exit.

"I heard the sous chef is swamped because of it," another said.

I was close to the exit when I saw Arielle poke her head out of her office.

"Do we have an update?"

No answer.

"People." Her pretty eyes darted from left to right. "Anyone? *Who* has an update for me? Charm? Someone tell me something."

"We've called around for backup," her assistant, Charmaine, voiced as she took quick steps toward Arielle. "But nothing yet."

Arielle's eyes met mine for only a moment before she focused on Charmaine again.

"Keep me posted. I *need* an update in the next five minutes. No later. Keep calling around. I'll do the same."

Arielle had disappeared into her office when I yawned and lifted my wrist to check my watch.

I was off the clock, but they seemed to need the help.

I was also tired as hell, but I'd never—at least in the three days working at *The St. James* — seen it be this chaotic.

I was in front of Arielle's door, tapping my knuckles on the mahogany surface.

She had her office phone to her ear when she lifted one finger, signaling for me to wait.

"Chef André has the flu." She sighed into the phone. "The sous chef is overwhelmed, and the evening rush is starting in less than an hour. Do you have anyone who—"

"I can step in," I said from the door.

She stared at me for a moment before lowering the phone to press it to her chest. "Pardon me?"

"I can step in for Chef André."

Her brows wrinkled even more.

I lifted my arm to lean my weight against her doorframe. "I did a stint at Nobu as a line cook. Two years at The Modern—garde manger to grill station. Plus, prep work at GrayArea, Daniel—"

"No," she interjected.

I arched both brows. "No?"

"No," she repeated. "This is *The St. James*. It's not a corner bar." She lifted her phone to her ear again. "Yes, I'm back. Where was I?"

I folded my bottom lip into my mouth, running my top teeth over it, smirking to myself.

"What do you mean you have no one for me—"

"Let me help you," I said again from the door.

She looked up from her desk, the phone still to her ear. "Didn't I already tell you no?"

I pushed myself off the doorframe and made my way into her office.

"Let me handle this, then call you back," she said low into the phone before returning it to its base.

"From where I was standing, it doesn't sound like you have many options, Arielle."

"*Ms.* St. James," she corrected.

I smiled. "My bad... *Ms. St. James.*"

She held her stare with me.

"Now, I've only been here for three days, but the restaurant's evening crowd seem to pour in at this hour. Plus, this time during the week, you don't want to have any more hiccups than what you're dealing with now."

Her beautiful eyes darted along my face.

"So, let me help y'all out," I tried again, pressing my hand to my chest. "And if I'm trash, you can fire me before dessert."

She twisted her lips to one side, biting the inside of her cheek. Exhaled a breath while closing her eyes for only a moment.

"A line cook at Nobu," she recalled.

"Nobu. The Modern. GrayArea. Daniel," I reiterated. "It's all on my résumé. I lied about none of it."

A deep breath that swelled her chest later, she exhaled once more, "One dish and, *God help you*, Micah..." She shook her head. "Do *not* disappoint me."

———

I went right to work the moment I stepped into *The St. James Table's* kitchen. I moved from station to station, introducing myself, tasting everything, making suggestions, then getting to work myself.

The top two buttons on my shirt were unbuttoned, sleeves already rolled up, black gloves on hands. Eyes burning like you wouldn't believe.

I peeked up a few times to survey the kitchen, tired eyes falling on a junior line cook who was staring at a bubbling sauce in a pan, nervous as hell.

"Kev, right?" I called out.

"Yeah, Micah?"

"You aight over there?"

"To be real? I don't know. I... I think I split the sauce—"

"Turn the heat down," I said to him. "Add a little cold cream. Slowly." I gestured with my hand. "Don't rush. We got time."

"Got it."

I leaned over the steel counter just enough to drag a blackberry gastrique into a crescent curve, placing the rib I'd glazed on the plate like it belonged there.

"Table nine," the expeditor called out. "One short rib, one vegan pasta, fire now!"

Without removing my eyes off what I was working on, I said, "James, you're on pasta. You've done it twice tonight." I nodded, turning to get more of the sauce. "Keep it tight." Then I tossed a look to my left. "Darius, was it?"

Darius nodded from feet away. "Yessir."

"Give me a rib on the fly. I'll plate."

I lifted my eyes for only a moment to make sure Darius heard what I said, and was working on it, when I did a double take at Arielle watching from the pass—the area in the kitchen where finished dishes are placed for servers to pick up and deliver to patrons. Hard to miss her, too. Standing there, silent. Still.

I smiled to myself, shaking my head. She was watching me like a correctional officer and I couldn't tell if it was in awe or because she was waiting for me to do the thing she told me not to do... disappoint her. Either way, I made a mental note to give her a good show.

"Micah," the sous chef, Rafi, said beside me. "You ever run a kitchen before, man?"

I chuckled, eyes down on the plate I was working on. "I've run plenty of kitchens. Just never wanted to stay in one... unless it was mine."

He laughed. "Well, this might just be yours then, 'cause you're killin' it, for real."

The dish I was working on came together fast—sweet potato whip, the rib placed perfectly, sauce dragged in a clean crescent. I wanted to eat it myself.

I slid the plate to the runner. "Table seven. VIP table. And yo..." I motioned for him to lean in. "Walk like it's yours, aight?"

He laughed and nodded. "I got you."

My attention moved to Arielle again, to see her in the same spot, eyes still on me. I could feel her fixed attention, and I liked it a lot.

I was in the kitchen for another hour when the orders finally started to slow. Cooks were still moving with ease, tickets still coming in and going out.

"*Uh*, Chef Micah?" I heard from a few feet in front of me. I knew the flirty voice before my eyes met the speaker.

I snorted a laugh.

"What's up, Leah?" I asked *The St. James* restaurant hostess, lifting my eyes to hers.

She wore a big smile and gestured behind her. "The woman at the VIP table—the one you made that special dish for? The short rib? She'd like to speak with you."

My chest tightened. A patron asking for the chef could mean a lot of things. But Leah was smiling, so maybe... it was good.

I wiped my hands on my apron, adjusted it, and followed the hostess to the table, where I was met with smiles, compliments, and handshakes.

And of course, Arielle wasn't far behind to witness it all.

"What you've done with this is incredible," the VIP patron boasted, her cheeks glowing from blushing in her seat. "You curated an entire experience. But I'm sure you know that."

I laughed, pressing my hand to my chest. "Thank you."

"No, *please*, thank *you*." She motioned at her plate. "I thoroughly enjoyed this masterpiece you've called a meal. From my first bite to the last. Exceptional."

It was near the restaurant's closing time when I decided to call it a night. Any other time, I would've offered to stay and help clean up, but I'd been on my feet since noon. It was after midnight, and I was running on only a few hours of sleep. There wasn't anything or anyone waiting for me at home that was as exciting as the praise I'd received tonight, but I needed my bed.

So after bidding good night to the cooks, sous chef, and restaurant staff, I made my way through *The St. James* main floor.

On my way to the exit, through the hotel's late-night quiet, I thought of the oxygen tank's hum back at home. A different kind of rhythm, a different kind of quiet. And the weight in my chest pressed heavier than it had in *The St. James Table* kitchen. This time, it ached too.

The compliments still echoing in my memory lightened that a little, making a tired smile pull at the corners of my mouth.

I was only feet away from the exit when I heard, "Good night, Micah."

I turned to the voice, spotting Arielle leaning against the doorframe of her office's entrance, where her assistant sat. Arielle's hands were in her trousers' pockets, her vibe calm and very sexy.

As opposed to that afternoon, when she was dressed in her usual tailor-made suit, the blazer was missing. She stood there in a pair of high-waisted, cinched-waist trousers with a silk cami tucked in. The cami teased a very enticing cleavage.

God, she's so beautiful.

I turned to face her, keeping my distance.

"Ms. St. James," I said back, then tilted my head to one side, a teasing grin forming on my lips. "Did *you* need something?"

She released a scoffing laugh and shook her head. "Just saying good night... and thank you... for assisting us tonight."

I smiled. "You're very welcome. Does that mean I didn't disappoint you?"

"You didn't," she answered. "I was quite satisfied by how much of a star you were in my kitchen."

"You look surprised by that."

Her lips curved a bit at the sides of her mouth, almost revealing a smile. "Because I am."

With that, she turned and entered her office area, closing the door behind her.

And I couldn't help but smile even bigger at the fact that I cracked the ice between us.

Not a huge break, more like a hairline fracture, but fuck it... it was something I could *definitely* work with.

DAY 7: LOSE YOUR GRIP

ARIELLE

It's like I had no control over my eyes anymore. My feet either. Because for another day, I stood outside *Vesper*, our rooftop lounge, peering through the glass at Micah.

I lifted the folder of invoices I'd been pretending to review for the past twenty minutes. Leafing through the pages, my eyes returned—every other second—to peering through the damn glass at our bartender.

Day 7 was no easier than the first day I met him.

There was just something about him that I couldn't quite put my finger on or ignore.

Something good. Really good.

The obvious would be that he was smooth. Confident. Spoke so easily to our guests who often liked to keep to themselves up here. Our guests were discerning, valued discretion. Quiet. But with Micah, they were open to his commanding, confident nature. I could relate.

"Oh," I heard in front of me. I lifted my eyes to spot another one of the restaurant staff from *The St. James Table* approaching the glass door. "Hi, Ms. St. James."

"Hello, Tania," I greeted.

She smiled, lighting up, like all the others did. Pleased, I'm sure, that I knew who they were and remembered their name. It was always the cutest reaction to witness. Little did they know, I made it a priority to know the names of every employee that called *The St. James* their job. I learned very young that people's names were the sweetest sound. Something that belonged to them, but they happily let others use.

A fact my ex-husband Julian still struggled with. He seemed to relish any opportunity to remind a subordinate they were just that.

I never saw the point in that. People worked better when they felt like part of a team—not like they were standing outside of one.

Tania opened the glass door and made her way to the bar, like all her other colleagues. Some were still hanging out there. Pulling Micah into conversation whenever he wasn't serving a patron.

He was Mr. Popular ever since his performance in *The St. James Table* kitchen.

Not a boy. A man that I still couldn't figure out my pull to.

Because I'd mocked my father for chasing younger women. I'd rolled my eyes at Julian and his wife, Karmen, who was twenty years his junior. But now... what the hell was I doing? Making excuses to be near a bartender thirteen years younger than me.

I was standing outside the bar, convincing myself that I was watching him to manage morale. But as much as I told myself that, the more I knew it was a lie. Especially with my father's voice still floating in my conscience about it.

My heels clicked against the stone floors as I made my way through the front door of my father's triplex. I'd called this place my home for seventeen years of my life, even though it's never really felt like home.

I could smell the earthy stench of Scotch in the air from the front door.

I followed the echoes of my father's laughter into the great room. Found him on the couch, Scotch in hand, phone to his ear, his ankle resting on his knee as he spoke softly into the phone like some kind of Casanova.

"Dad," I said, placing my bag on a nearby table. "Do you have a moment?"

He peeked over the neck of the couch at me and sighed.

"Evelyn, my love, I'll have to call you back," he voiced into the phone. "I know, I know. I'll call you back in a moment, my sweets. My daughter has just walked in and by the tone of her voice, I can tell I'm in trouble."

I rolled my eyes as he chuckled at his own words.

His assistant had just told me about Evelyn and how my father had been flying her to Italy and back on a whim whenever his new thirty-something girlfriend wanted.

I made my way around the couch to take a seat in the plush armchair across from him.

"And to what do I owe the pleasure of this visit?"

"The fishing resort in Montauk," I got to it, crossing my legs. "Care to explain?"

"Not really."

"Miles and Langston—"

"Are hugely supportive of the endeavor," he interjected, gesturing with his Scotch in hand. "They're looking forward to what will come of it."

"Of course they are," I mumbled.

I closed my eyes for only a moment, inhaling an encouraging breath.

As always, Miles and Langston played the supportive role while putting me in front to parent our parent.

"It doesn't make sense financially, Dad," I insisted. "You know that."

"What I know is..." He sat up in his seat. "I taught you every-

thing you know, kid. And so, I'm more than capable of making decisions that don't have to involve your input or critique."

My eyes moved to the fireplace, where a photo of my mother, Robin St. James, still sat on the polished mantel. Because she was actually the one who taught me everything. No sense in correcting my father though

"The decision is questionable at best." I refocused on my father. "Where you are choosing to waste the family's resources, is concerning."

He scoffed.

"Your investment in this spot in Montauk," I started. "This new thing you have going on with a woman several decades younger than you—"

"Now that is simply none of your business, now is it?"

I pressed my lips together and inhaled a slow breath.

"You can't begin to understand men like me, Ari, so do yourself a favor and don't even start," he gritted out. The laugh lines carved into his deep brown skin only seemed to deepen with the smugness in his tone. "You've always been too stiff, too rigid when it comes to relationships. Since you need me to spell it out... I'm courting, kid."

"Courting?" I scoffed. "You're splurging on a woman who is more than half your age and younger than your daughter."

He stared at me for a moment, a smirk appearing on his lips.

"I find it comical that you're making age a concern this morning."

I wrinkled my brows.

"Julian tells me you've got your own little boytoy now. The bartender?"

I swallowed hard.

"The one you let run your kitchen?"

"He didn't run anything," I snapped. "He stepped in. Our head chef called out last minute with the flu—"

"And you left such a privileged opportunity to the cute rooftop bartender? Was the sous chef not qualified enough?"

"The sous chef was overwhelmed," I said, holding my composure.

"Micah, the bartender, has experience. More experience than the sous—"

"Does he now?"

His questioning sent my pulse racing, because I didn't like the implication.

"I run a respectable brand," I ground out. "I would never in this lifetime or the next leave my brand in the hands of a child to run because I thought he was cute."

"Well..." My father leaned back in his seat, tossing back his Scotch. "We all have done crazy things for a pretty face, Ari." He lifted his glass in the air at me. "So welcome to the fold... cradle robber. And do be sure to hold all judgment from here on out."

His words were still in mind as I stood outside of *Vesper* for another day. Because as much as I tried to tell myself I was up outside our rooftop bar managing morale and reviewing invoices, I couldn't lie that my motivation for being there... was Micah. *All him.*

"Knew I'd find you here," Julian said behind me.

I tensed up, then immediately inhaled a breath to relax my shoulders before I turned to face him. "I was just... leaving, actually."

"Were you?"

He smiled, his eyes focusing past me and through the glass doors.

"Every time I call your office, Charmaine informs me you're away from your desk."

I tilted my head to one side.

"And every time I ask around regarding your whereabouts, staff always says you're up here, as of late." He folded his arms over his wide chest. "Should I thank him?"

I furrowed my brows. "Thank *who*?"

"Micah." He smirked, the sun cutting through the sleek glass panels, bouncing off his russet brown skin. "That's his name, right?"

"Thank him for what?"

"Keeping you so preoccupied with him that I haven't heard about that *little* meeting you promised we'd be having."

I kissed my teeth and turned to gather my papers.

"You've been ignoring my texts about the Birkin."

"Is it disappointing that I haven't let it get under my skin as you probably would have enjoyed?"

He chuckled, and I rolled my eyes.

Nine years of marriage. Divorced for only one year, and I felt like Julian was a complete stranger to me.

My father put us together. And by put, I *mean* put. Julian's father was an entrepreneur and a big player in the premium liquor space, so of course, my father was intrigued by that—being the functional drunk he was. And there I was, a newly minted 31, unmarried, and simply wanting to check marriage off my to-dos. It was good the first five years, but then things got problematic. Julian's eyes started to wander by year six. Other parts of him by year eight. By year nine, he was complaining about my lack of interest in being a pillow princess in bed for him, wanting to take charge. And it was then I realized there was someone else.

Karmen.

That, and me finding her in our bed when he thought I would be away on a business trip at our brand's hotel in London.

I ended it right then. Left our duplex and never returned after that night.

Ironically, I got more criticism for leaving than Julian ever did for cheating.

"I've spoken to him," my dad said after I told him why I was leaving the duplex. "He's sorry, feels terrible. But you tapped out too soon, Ari. You're tougher than this. Men will be men—you've got to understand that. He still loves you."

Yeah. Loved me so much he proposed and married his mistress before the ink on our divorce papers could dry well enough to spite me for leaving instead of forgiving. And he *still* had the nerve to call what they had love.

After ending things with Julian, I stayed at *The St. James* for a week. Bought my penthouse and started over. That was a year ago.

And that was never the plan. Divorce. But... here we were.

I cradled the papers in my hand and turned to face him again. "I've been enjoying these last few days of not seeing you and thought I'd continue treating myself to your absence since it was going *so* well."

He stared at me for a moment, attention moving through the glass again.

"You should sleep with him... get it out of your system before he starts thinking he matters."

I blinked hard, swallowed the knot forming in my throat. Julian's eyes met mine again. He licked his lips slowly and took a step closer to me.

"Maybe he's the one to crack the ice queen act," he whispered. "Because Lord knows I couldn't... although sometimes I miss how much of a kink I made that challenge into."

I clenched my jaw.

"I don't know." He shrugged. "Maybe the young bartender will have just as much *fun* trying like I did. Hopefully he'll have more gusto and patience, because I simply couldn't hang any longer."

"Fuck you, Julian."

"Oh, believe me, I'd *love* to, Ari," he retorted then bit his bottom lip. "But I don't think *my wife* would be okay with that. Apparently wives don't approve of such behavior with other women. Even if it's just once and didn't even last long. Right or wrong?"

I scoffed in disgust. "Get out of my face. Now."

He chuckled lowly while stepping back and turning to leave the area.

And as I watched him walk away, I moved my eyes through the glass door once more, my gaze meeting Micah's before I pulled my attention away.

Julian wrecked me a little with his *you should sleep with him* remark. Not because what he said was crude, but because it was cruel... and kind of close to something I wanted but would never admit to myself, much less let myself do.

———

Later that evening, after *The St. James Table* was closed, I made my way there to sit at the wood bar alone and enjoy the dim quiet.

I unlocked the door, stepped inside, and ran my hand over the black velvet sofa near the entrance. I was just steps away from the bar when I spotted a shadow to my right.

Tucked away in one of the armchairs by the bar was Micah, sitting and reading.

He saw me when I saw him.

"Good night, Ms. St. James."

I only realized I'd been holding onto my breath when I finally exhaled deeply.

"Good night... Micah." I lifted my wrist. "Thought you were supposed to have been gone hours ago."

"The sous chef wanted me to share my short rib recipe." He nodded. "Then he had some other questions—"

"I'm not paying you overtime for that, Micah," I cut in.

"Never asked you to," he replied, smoothly. Unfazed. Micah lifted the book he'd been reading when I walked in. "I decided to hang back after everyone left because I like the vibe in here. The silence. It isn't eerie. It's like... quiet luxury... or something."

I had to contain my reaction. That was literally my goal for *The St. James*. One I've *never* shared with anyone... but he understood it without being told. How creepy... in a good way. I could've listened to him talk all day—just realized that. His cadence was so relaxed, sometimes rhythmical. He had a baritone with a little gravel. Not too rough, just... lived-in.

Way too much soul for a 28-year-old.

"Do you have ID?"

His brows rose high above his eyes. "ID?"

"Yes." I approached, leaning an arm against the lip of the bar. "I realized I never asked to see it. I'm sure you gave it to HR for your new hire paperwork, but I've never seen it."

"May I ask why you're asking now, then?"

"I want to confirm your age."

A smile bloomed on his lips. "Do you think I'm lying about my age, Ms. St. James?"

I licked my lips and looked away.

"Do you think I'm younger than what I've told you?"

"I think you're older."

He folded his bottom lip into his mouth, then dragged his teeth over it. It was something I've seen him do once or twice before—and every time he did it, it stole my breath just a little.

He stood from his seat, dipped his hand into the back pocket of his black slacks, and pulled out a wallet as he approached. Beside me, he placed his ID on the bar's counter.

Micah Black. October 24, 1996.

1996 was the year I turned 13, finishing my last year in middle school.

I released a scoffing laugh to myself.

"Satisfied?" he asked beside me.

I offered a single nod. "Thank you."

"Your turn to show me yours," he said.

When I turned to glance at him again, the grin he wore was cunning, lowkey—and God help me, it made me laugh.

He stared at me for a moment, eyes unwavering.

"You have a very beautiful laugh," he commented. "Beautiful smile, too. You should let it out more often."

I tucked my lips into my mouth, slowly releasing them, and his eyes watched it all happen before he met my gaze again.

"There hasn't been a reason to let it out more often."

His smirk returned, and then he shrugged. "I don't know why that feels like a challenge I'd like to accept."

It was quiet in *The St. James Table*. With staff gone, the

kitchen closed, silence was the only thing to fill the space between our words.

I dropped my gaze to the book he'd placed on the bar when he came over.

"*L'Étranger*," he said, lifting the book to give me a better look of it. "It's slow going, but it sticks better when I read it out loud."

I blinked in response.

"It's about this guy who doesn't feel anything... until it's too late," he added. "It's frustrating and brilliant. Makes you wonder how much you're pretending just to survive."

"*Hmph*," I responded, his words sinking in a bit more than I expected.

He chuckled. "I'm reading it mostly for the French. You wanna hear me butcher some words and sentences?"

I released a small laugh. "That's all right. You've already outperformed my expectations this week."

"That sounds dangerously close to a compliment." He leaned an arm on the bar, his eyes never leaving mine. "Be careful. It might land one of these days."

My lips twitched into a smile. "Don't get used to it."

I didn't know what it was about Micah, but he made me feel comfortable around him.

With everyone else, there was always this need for them to perform—or to please me.

And I wasn't much better. I always felt the need to assert my authority. To stay in control.

But with him... I didn't feel like I had to do any of that.

He was just flowing. Reciprocating energy. It was strangely refreshing. Humanizing—and unexpectedly relaxing.

His eyes did a slow crawl from my eyes to my lips before refocusing again. "You smile when you talk to me."

"Do I?"

"*Mmm-hmm*," he replied with a nod. Micah placed a little more weight on the arm on the bar. "Not quite all the way. But it's there. Like something you don't want to show too much of but can't hold back either."

For a moment, I forgot where we were. Because as he stood beside me, closer than when he first approached, I didn't feel like recoiling or creating space between us. I wanted to eliminate it. Lean more into his warmth... because that's how it felt in his presence... like bathing in sunlight.

At first, during his interview, I thought it was all in my head. But it's been like this every time.

I exhaled and didn't look away. I didn't want to.

Because Micah's warmth melted something in me. And even though I didn't like the thought of it, I *loved* how it felt.

His eyes bored into me, head tilting. "You ever think about just... letting it happen?"

"Letting what happen?" I asked, low.

"Whatever *this* is."

Under his gaze, I was weightless... and it was weird. Because I'd only known him for seven days, and a part of me felt like I'd known him forever.

His question hung between us. I shifted a little on my heels, and the movement brought me closer to Micah. So close, my hand brushed his by accident, pooling heat between my thighs like a slow burning blaze. My eyes dropped to our hands then shot to his dark brown eyes before my attention lowered to his mouth —thick two-toned lips that appeared to be so soft, I could feel them from a distance.

Curiosity made me wonder. Gall had me actually closing the distance. Because yes... I *had* thought about just letting it happen. So much so, I didn't stop moving until my lips brushed against his.

And he didn't delay, but he wasn't hasty either, pressing his mouth flush against mine.

For a moment, I was not there, in reality. I was somewhere else. Just me and Micah. In a kiss that started off gentle, like I was testing the security of it. And he didn't rush me or deepen it. Not yet at least.

He let me lead. Not in a yielding way. Graciously. Only parting his lips when I parted mine. Only caressing my tongue with his when I caressed his with mine.

My hand lifted to his chest when his arm circled my waist, pulling me closer to him.

A low moan escaped his lips, causing an immediate reaction beneath my waist. That region pulsed now with a sensation I hadn't felt in a year. Shit... who am I kidding? I've *never* felt *this*.

His hand brushed the side of my face and I melted against his touch, completely out of my control. In that instant, I started to feel *everything* in his embrace... too damn much at one time.

My eyes shot open. I pressed my hand firmly against his chest, using the leverage to pull back—breaking the kiss by just an inch.

That same hand flew to my mouth a second later, grounding me back in reality.

Micah had left me breathless.

I couldn't get control of my pulse. Or my breathing.

"That was a mistake," I said, my voice low. Breaking.

Micah slowly dragged his finger along the curve of his mouth.

"Aight," he said softly. "I'm still glad you just let it happen."

I dropped my attention from him. Swallowed hard. Created more space between us.

My pulse was in my ears, getting louder the farther I stepped back from him.

I stared at him, watching him stand cool and collected—and the vision had me wanting to return to my position in front of him. Maybe even on the bar counter this time, knowing he'd know exactly how to relieve the pressure building between my thighs.

I have to get out of here.

"Good night, Micah."

He licked his lips slowly, then offered a single nod. "Good night... Ms. St. James."

I turned and walked away—as composed, but as quickly as possible. My heels tapped softly on the hardwood, breaking the silence that lingered before all of what happened.

I felt outside myself. Untethered. Off script.

I turned to glance over my shoulder, for what, I didn't know. To see where I'd left my sanity, maybe. Definitely not to see Micah still standing in the spot I left him. Hands in his pockets, just calmly watching me leave.

My lips were tingling by the time I got to *The St. James Table's* exit. My heart steady. Barely. Head spinning.

I just kissed the damn bartender.

What the hell were you thinking, Ari?!

And why didn't I want it to be a one-time thing?

DAY 10: LOSE YOUR ARMOR

MICAH

"M icah," my patron, Alani, said in front of me. She lifted her martini glass and smiled over the rim of it. "I just love the way your name *feels* in my mouth. *Micah*."

I suppressed my laugh as I pressed my hands onto the counter in front of her.

"Do you have a girlfriend, Micah?"

It was near the end of my shift in *Vesper*, early evening. I'd been there since early afternoon... and so had this patron.

She'd leave for hours, then reappear in the same seat—flirting like she never left.

Cute, but not distracting.

"I don't have a girlfriend," I answered.

"You should have a girlfriend... Micah."

This time, I chuckled and licked my lips.

Alani had too many of these Cosmopolitans. In fact, too many was had two glasses ago. She was on a work trip, had plans to attend a conference in a couple of days. She lived in Arizona but traveled to New York because her company had offices here.

Alani, like many of my lady patrons, told me everything—often too much—over the glasses of drinks I mixed for them. Most kept it casual. But some, like Alani, were flirty drinkers.

I was still trying to figure out a woman who wasn't a patron but who I wished showed the kind of attention Alani was giving me so easily.

Arielle St. James.

Then again, I'm not sure I would be as drawn to Arielle if she were like Alani. I kind of loved the chase, the challenge Arielle posed by being so... *her*.

A soft hand being placed atop mine pulled me out of my head and back behind the bar at *Vesper*.

I peeked down to see Alani's manicured nails tracing the veins on the back of my hand. My gaze lifted in time to see her staring at me with glossy eyes.

"Room 224," she said, her words slow to come out of her mouth. "That's where you can find me, okay... Micah?"

I inhaled a deep breath as she stood from her stool. She threw back the rest of her drink and slinked away, her heels an arch-nemesis to her balance as she headed to the exit. Alani switched her hips nice and slow as she left, throwing a glance over her shoulder at me.

And all I could do was release a scoffing laugh.

I wouldn't be going. Beyond it being unprofessional and a crazy ass risk—even if Alani was a beautiful woman in her late twenties like me—she wasn't who I had on my mind.

I'd been thinking about that kiss between Arielle and me since it happened. She'd been avoiding me ever since. Her office door, usually cracked open, stayed shut like it had something to protect.

Usually, when I arrived for my shift, her office door would be open. Sometimes her assistant wasn't nearby to stop me from approaching, giving me a chance to stay top of mind by saying good afternoon.

But that opportunity had been interfered with. Arielle had been keeping that damn door closed.

It had been three days since that kiss. And for three days, that kiss had been the first thing I thought about in the morning and the last thing I tried to forget before I went to sleep.

The glass door of the bar opened, drawing my attention to it. I half-expected for Alani to return, like she'd been doing all day, but instead I spotted someone I usually didn't see around here.

Julian Carmichael.

The day I was scheduled to interview for the bartending position, his assistant called to confirm that I would be meeting with him. I was shocked when I didn't and met with Arielle instead. And thank God for that, because something told me had it been Julian I met with, I wouldn't have stepped another foot behind this counter. I've had only a few interactions with Julian. Too few to count. He didn't like me. I could tell by the way he looked at me through his squinted glares from a distance. He'd never actually stepped onto the rooftop bar since I've gotten here. So his arrival today was... different.

"Micah, correct?" he said, taking a seat at the center bar. "I don't think we've been formally introduced."

"No, sir." I nodded once. "But I know who you are, Mr. Carmichael."

"Good," he said next, his eyes floating past me to survey the bar. "Pour me a Scotch. Neat."

Of course. It's like I said, the people who often frequented the bar, always kept it predictable. Stuffy. Much like themselves.

At his request, I poured him up his drink, placing a *Vesper* labeled napkin in front of him, followed by his drink.

"Very good," he commented, lifting his drink and immediately taking a sip.

I was turning away, mainly to find something to do when he said, "Surprised to see Ms. St. James not up here."

I focused on him. "Sorry, what was that?"

"Ms. St. James." He smirked, lifted his glass again to sip. "She seems to have found the view up here to be more interesting than her office lately... since *you've* arrived, at least."

I turned completely to face him. There had been some talk about Arielle and Julian. Staff had already shared that they were once a couple. Very few said they were in love. Only married and now divorced. I never cared to probe further than that.

"Can I get you anything else, Mr. Carmichael?"

He grinned and swirled the Scotch in his glass. "A man of discretion. You're tactful, Micah. I can respect that... even if it's inconvenient."

Julian finished his drink and stood to his feet. "I'd be careful, though, flying so close to the sun with wax wings. Mortals rarely survive that fall... regardless of how *tactful* or *discreet* they are."

I blinked in response, trying my hardest not to show what I was feeling... annoyed.

"Look, I'll be frank with you, Micah. Ms. St. James may seem like an enticing conquest, but, come on... you'd be punching way above your weight class if you even tried." He chuckled, smooth and smug. "She has a type, like *most* women do." He twisted his diamond watch, adjusted the collar on his expensive dress shirt next. "Rich is her type, if that wasn't clear enough for you—"

"As it should be, sir," I cut in, pressing my hands onto the bar counter, refusing to change face. "A woman with her class should always aspire for rich. But I would imagine for a woman who has it all, the *rich* she wants? Doesn't exactly come with a price tag attached, feel me?"

"Do I *feel* you?" He laughed, loudly. "No, Micah, I don't feel *that*. Because what other rich is there? *Please*. Enlighten me."

"Rich in traits of excellence, sir."

His humor slowly faded from his lips.

"Like honor, respect." I held eye contact without blinking. "Integrity, to name a select few. Rich in character and morals, which seems to be a rarity around her since she might be surrounded by people who are piss poor in character and morally bankrupt... sir."

He stared at me for a moment, scoffing lowly a second later.

"The vodka needs refilling," he said, turning on his designer loafers to leave. "Make sure you handle that before your shift ends."

"Will do, Mr. Carmichael," I said to his back.

Fucking jackass, I thought to myself as I tracked him with my eyes until he was out of sight.

All that money, and he still couldn't buy class.

I turned to pull down the bottle of vodka. "No surprise he's the ex."

The bar was quiet after that, patrons likely in *The St. James Table*, ordering dinner and drinks at their bar like they often did at this hour.

So I decided to take advantage of the quiet and low traffic.

Julian had put Arielle top of mind for me. That, and the kiss we'd shared at *The St. James Table* bar. Random as hell, but still a really good surprise. Her lips were as soft as they looked, but she was surprisingly softer in our kiss than I expected.

And I really liked that.

I wanted to see her and needed a reason to. So, I pulled out a shaker, dropped ice into it, then opened the mini fridge beneath the bar to grab grapefruit juice. I turned to the shelves and grabbed Reposado tequila and Aperol, immediately getting to work.

Used the tequila as my base before adding bitterness and spice with the Aperol, grapefruit juice, and smoked chili bitters. Added just enough agave to the shaker and gave the ingredients a shake before straining it into a coupe glass. I garnished it with a flamed grapefruit peel, then carefully lifted the glass, grabbed a *Vesper*-branded napkin, and made my way down.

Just as I expected, Arielle's office door was closed. And it was just my luck her assistant was missing.

I stood there for only a breath, hesitating. Up at the bar, this seemed like a good idea, but down here in front of the closed door, I was second guessing myself. I ran my tongue beneath my top lip, Julian's comment playing in the back of my mind.

Ms. St. James may seem like an enticing conquest, but, come on… you'd be punching way above your weight class if you even tried.

Rich is her preference.

"Fuck it," I muttered, then tapped a rhythm on her door and waited.

"Yes?" she asked from the other side.

"It's Micah."

I swallowed hard at the too-long silence that lingered after I made myself known.

My few seconds of worry dissipated when I heard, "Come in, Micah."

Arielle's eyes were already searching for mine before I could get the door open all the way.

I kept a smile on my lips though and refused to break eye contact first.

Her eyes left mine when she lowered them to see the glass in my hand.

"For you," I said, setting it down on her desk.

"I didn't order this."

Short. Snappy. It all just made it so hard not to smile at.

"You didn't," I confirmed. "But I figured you could use it."

She leaned back in her office chair and folded her arms over her tailored blazer. "Oh?"

"It's called Control Issues." I pushed my hands into my black slacks. "Felt like it fit you."

She jerked her head back first, closed her eyes next, then let a laugh escape her lips.

"Aren't you bold?" she asked, low. "And a little presumptuous."

Once the humor faded, a smile remained on her face—and melted me right where I stood.

"My boldness has nothing on that smile, though," I exhaled, eyes still locked with hers.

"The same smile that led to you having your tongue in my mouth."

I coughed, then laughed in response, getting another giggle from her.

I held a hand up in front of me. "I apologize—"

"Don't," she interjected. "You didn't do anything wrong. *I* kissed *you*, remember?"

"I really don't remember who did what." I shrugged. "I've been wanting to do it for so long, I'm surprised you beat me to it."

She tried to hide her smile by balling her lips together, but failed terribly.

"Micah, this is extremely inappropriate—"

"Taste it." I gestured at the drink, hoping to shift focus. "During my interview you challenged me to make a drink you'd like, knowing little about you. Here's another one. Tell me I'm right about you, boss lady."

She stared at me for a moment, then focused on the drink. Inhaled a deep breath, then lifted it. Arielle sipped. A quiet moan slipped past her lips.

"Wow," she whispered first, then adjusted her voice. "This is... wow."

She glanced at me over the rim of her glass. 'This is really good, Micah... possibly one of the best drinks I've ever had. Thank you."

"You're welcome... Ms. St. James."

She lowered the glass, smiling. "Micah, you know what my tongue tastes like. You don't have to call me Ms. St. James."

I smirked. "Just following your rules."

"Do you *always* follow rules?"

"Only until I'm told to break them."

Her jaw slacked a little, eyes locked onto mine, chest rising. Once. Then again.

It was when I licked my lips that she broke eye contact, running her hand down her neck and inhaling a deep breath.

I smiled at that.

"*Uh...*" She shifted in her seat and tried again. "That... *umm...* shit."

I chuckled lowly. She was flustered. That was *so* sexy.

"The... a... VIP guest," she forced out. "The one you made the short ribs for keeps calling me for 'the good looking chef' daily."

My brows shot up. "Really?"

"She returned last night and our sous chef, Rafi, prepared the short ribs for her." She pointed. "Rafi said he got the recipe from you?"

I nodded. "I gave it to him."

"Well, Ms. VIP said while it was good... the short ribs weren't *your* short ribs."

My heart leapt at that.

"And now *I* wish I requested one of those ribs that night."

"I can make it for you. Tonight."

I don't know why I said that. It was impulsive. Audacious. Inappropriate, as she labeled my comment earlier... but I meant every word.

Maybe it was the kiss at *The St. James Table's* wooden bar. Maybe it was her ex flexing his ego unprovoked at *Vesper's* bar.

Whatever it was, I wanted *every* opportunity to share space with her. She deserved... and so did I.

Arielle shook her head and fanned her hand in the air. "*The St. James Table* closes in a few minutes. My private chef comes to my home in a few days. You can just... give me the recipe—"

"But it won't be *my* short ribs," I cut in.

She focused on me.

"You've already seen what happens when someone else tries to recreate my creation." I curved a slow smile. "If you want the *real thing*, Ms. St. James... you need the original. You need *me*."

She leaned back in her seat, brushed her finger over her top lip —painted red today—thinking.

I lifted my wrist to check the time. "I get off in half an hour. When I'm done, I can stop by the market, pick up what I need." I gestured at her next. "You can text me your address and I'll be there tonight to make my clearly world-famous short ribs."

"Micah—"

"I'll only cook for you," I interjected. "Leave right after. I swear. Aight?"

She released a scoffing laugh while shaking her head.

"Come on, Ms. St. James." I let another grin tug at the corners of my mouth. "Let me cook for you. I promise you won't regret it."

She pressed her tongue into her cheek and looked off, blinking a couple of times before refocusing on me. "What's your phone number, again?"

————

"Welcome," she greeted the moment the elevator opened into her penthouse. "Come in."

I had to go through two building doormen to get up here. The first one was the actual doorman, the other was a gentleman who called himself the building's concierge, standing by the elevator when I arrived. He had to call Arielle before keying in the access code for the car to arrive at her penthouse.

Expensive. Private. Quiet.

Her penthouse was also sterile.

I made my way through the open-plan living room, the floor-to-ceiling windows doing the job of stealing my attention with their panoramic city view.

It was a lot of space for one person—so much space, my footsteps echoed around me. The penthouse was beautiful, of course. But too big. *Too* cold. Like a high-end hotel suite that never got lived in but photographed well. It looked like she curated every-thing... except comfort.

I entered the kitchen and whistled. "Damn. I could get lost in here."

The space was pristine and visibly unused. I placed the bags of groceries on the kitchen's marbled island. Lifted my gaze long enough to see Arielle still standing feet away.

I gestured at the island stool across from me. "Come sit, Ms. St. James." I smiled next. "Let me feed you."

Her blazer, and delicate gold jewelry, were long gone. Tailored slacks still on with a white cami, snug against her frame, tucked into the waistband.

"You can call me *Ari*," she said, sitting where I invited her to. "You're in my home now. You can call me Ari. Everyone I know does."

I smiled and nodded. "Aight... *Ari*."

She moved her eyes off mine, licked her lips in an attempt to hold her smile back.

We spent the time filling silence with conversation. She told me about her private chef.

"I hired her because she's easy to talk to," Arielle revealed. "She reminds me of my mother."

I told her why I'm learning French.

"I wanna live in France for a bit. Study at Le Cordon Bleu."

And while the food simmered, and comfort was established between us, she asked me something I never expected.

"Are you single?"

"A little late to ask me that, no?"

She squeezed her eyes closed, and I laughed.

"I *am*... single."

"Why?"

"*Hmm...*" I stepped back, balancing my weight on my hands on the counter behind me. "I have a lot on my plate right now that makes me feel unstable. I'm not really rooted anywhere right now. Not enough for something real to grow." I paused, then glanced at her. "So, I'm single because I haven't found anyone who makes me want to stop moving and place down roots to watch something grow."

She nodded, her face soft, eyes too. "Very mature reply."

"And you?"

"Well, *I'm* single because I'm divorced." She nodded. "My business partner, Julian and I were married for almost a decade." She bit at her bottom lip. "And when you're with someone that long, it's a little difficult to put yourself back out there at my age."

"*Your* age." I quirked a smile. "Which is...?"

She smiled, and I chuckled, folding my bottom lip into my mouth to bite.

God, her smile.

"Why'd you two decide to end things?" I asked instead.

"*He* decided to end things when he had an affair with his now-wife."

I cringed.

So, *that's* what everyone at the hotel had been hinting at every time they mentioned that Arielle and Julian were married, but weren't anymore.

"Yeah." She fanned her hand in the air.

"I get it. No need to explain." I turned to the pot of sauce with plans to stir. "I heard you two were married, but wasn't told what happened. But even if I wasn't told about you two, I could tell y'all had history."

"How so?"

"Well," I turned to face her again. "He stopped by *Vesper* earlier, had some choice words for me."

She jerked her head back. "Did he?"

It was my turn to fan my hand in the air.

"Nothing I couldn't handle and definitely not worth getting into. Because aside from that, you always look tense around him, and he always looks pleased about that." I scoffed, shook my head. "Then there was the other day you two were speaking outside of the bar... when you were upstairs acting like you were working.

She released a short laugh. "I wasn't *acting*, Micah."

"Aight." I smirked. "Okay."

She rolled her eyes.

"It's humbling and very flattering that you notice me at all... Ari."

She blinked in response.

"So... you know, don't stop *working* outside of *Vesper*."

Arielle shook her head, then looked away.

After a few more minutes, the last of the food was done cooking.

I plated the whipped sweet potato, formed the beautiful blackberry gastrique crescent along one of her plates, and plated the ribs. White steam ribboned out of the plate when I slid it in front of her.

"The exact same VIP plate, just for you," I said. "Enjoy."

She used a knife and fork to cut a piece of the meat off. The cleanest way I've ever seen someone eat a rib. Such a refined and put-together woman who seemed like she kept a lot of things contained.

And it was that mystery that drew me to her. That mystery that had me staying after, cleaning up and conversing more with her.

"Next time," she said as I finished wiping the counter, "you'll have to make enough for yourself too."

"Next time?" I turned to face her. "Will there be a *next* time?"

"Maybe," she countered, her smile soft. "I don't see why not."

My smile was larger, blooming more from my chest than my lips.

"Aight." I nodded. "I'm looking forward to it."

In more ways than she would ever know.

And maybe next time, eating won't be my only reason to stay.

Maybe... she won't want for me to leave at all.

DAY 14: LOSE YOUR BOUNDARIES

ARIELLE

"So, you were right," I said, cutting into the asparagus on my plate.

Micah lifted his eyes from his plate, fixing his attention on me.

We sat in my kitchen, at the marble island, eating the meal he'd prepared on my stove.

Our second dinner. This time, he sat across from me—at my insistence.

"I gave your short rib recipe to my personal chef."

He licked his lips clean, setting his fork down.

"She followed it to the letter." I licked the corner of my mouth, needing to savor every bit of what he'd created tonight. "And *still*, it did *not* taste like yours."

As expected, all he did was nod. There was a beat of silence before he said, "Told you."

I released a breathy laugh, shaking my head.

His response wasn't cocky, although it had every right to be. Just matter-of-fact. Like always.

I was starting to understand him more now.

He was flirty, but subtly. Intuitively and quietly confident. He read people well—read me *so* well. And he had this ability to disarm with charm, never wasting his words. There was an edge to him, but he was also soft... and *incredibly* thoughtful.

After he made dinner at my home four days ago, he'd made it a habit to drop a drink off at my desk along with a note each day since.

Each day, either he or a server at *Vesper's lounge* would walk the drink over with a note listing the drink's name.

The second drink Micah brought—the day after dinner—was called High Functioning.

"For the woman who can do everything..." he'd said, placing the drink down on my desk, "...and still look perfect doing it." Micah turned for the door shortly after, instructing me to read the note.

I did, and laughed, alone in my office.

And the note?

A high-functioning cocktail for a high-functioning woman. Don't worry... this pairs well with delegation.
— MB.

It was delicious. An interesting mix with a vodka base, fresh lemon, and cucumber.

The next day, I'd been in and out of meetings, barely in my office. But when I returned, a new drink—this one darker, moodier—was waiting with another note.

Dark, deep, and something you didn't ask for, but won't stop thinking about.

I balled my lips to keep from smiling and kept reading.

There's no exit plan. Just sip and surrender.
— MB.

And so I did, rubbing my tongue along the roof of my mouth, savoring how the dark rum played with the black cherry syrup and orange bitters on my tongue. He'd even smoked a cinnamon stick for garnish. Figures. Smoking garnishes seemed to be his specialty.

By the third drink, I knew he was seducing me... in the best way.

I had just left a meeting and was heading out of the hotel for another when Charmaine told me I had a drink waiting on my desk. Her smirk was cute, but also concerning. I didn't want people talking... or knowing about Micah and me. Even when there wasn't much to know.

That concern didn't last once I stepped into my office and found the martini glass sitting pretty under my office lights with another note.

For the night when the craving isn't just for company,
but for something that actually lasts... because the
best things always do.
—MB.

He called it Worth the Wait. Cognac, honeyed pear syrup, splash of amaro. Of all the drinks, that one was my favorite. It's why I texted him on my way out of the hotel to ask when he was free to come by and cook dinner for me again—this time, for the both of us.

That was yesterday.

And tonight, he sat across from me—strong arms stretching

the sleeves of his black tee, taking the last few bites of the food, he made for us, looking as handsome as ever.

For everything I'd come to understand about him without him saying a word, he was still a mystery to me. And honestly, I think that's what I liked most about him.

"How'd you learn to cook like this?"

He lifted his gaze to mine.

"No formal training," I added. "Your only experience is assisting in notable kitchens—"

"I've got plenty of experience in kitchens you've never heard of."

I looked away, holding in my smile. It was responses like that I found so attractive about him.

"I had to learn to cook when I was real young." He nodded, placing his fork in his plate. "Didn't really have a choice. Some days I'd get home from school, starving. I hated school lunch, refused to eat it." He shrugged. "Besides curing hunger, cooking became the only place I could create something, you know? Where I had control..." He winked.

I released a scoffing laugh.

"...control over the outcome, the look—and that was cool, since I didn't have control anywhere else."

"Interesting," I said softly.

"I plan to get formal training one day—"

"One day isn't a day of the week."

He smiled, then licked his lips slowly. "When the time is right, I'd like to move to France. Paris. Study at Le Cordon Bleu. Hone my craft. I got my passport last year. Just waiting for the right time to get it stamped. I want France to be that first stamp."

"You'd be perfect there... in France. Le Cordon Bleu." I dabbed my napkin against my lips. "So, why delay? You're young, but you won't be forever."

He inhaled a deep breath, folded his bottom lip into his mouth, and ran his top teeth over it. After another beat of silence, he simply said...

"My dad..." He ran the tip of his tongue down the inside of his cheek. "He's *umm...*" He sighed, then leaned back in his seat. "He's dying."

I blinked hard in response, my hand flying to my chest.

"They gave him three months," he said with a slow nod. "That was almost a year ago." A brief smile touched his lips. "He's strong—always has been. But he's dying... and he's the *only* family I've got left, after my mom passed when I was fourteen. He said he wanted to die at home, so I turned his bedroom into a hospice. Asked his ex to be his nurse—she's there now. When I'm not at *The St. James*, I'm home. With him. Just... waiting. So... I *can't* leave." He swallowed hard then shook his head. "Not yet."

"Oh, Micah," I whispered, feeling my heart ache in my chest. "My God. I'm *so* sorry."

"Please." He raised a hand and shook his head. "Don't be."

I would have never guessed any of this. I knew there was a mysterious air to Micah, but this was the kind of heavy he didn't seem to be carrying.

"I also lost my mother when I was a teenager." I nodded. "When I was 16."

His eyes settled on mine.

I inhaled a deep breath and released it slowly.

"I never got to grieve her," I admitted. "Not properly... something I only realized after I got older. I didn't get the chance. On the limo ride back from the funeral, my father looked at me, nudged me playfully with his shoulder, and said, 'Well, Ari... you're up, kid.'"

Micah cringed, then closed his eyes.

I released a short laugh. "Yeah, he's the *best* with words. And at the time, I just... got to it."

Micah's brows furrowed.

"In hindsight, *I got to it* because playing the matriarch of my family was a distraction from the loss. So, I became the rock... a rock, really. Stone for everyone else's problems. Fixing without even thinking. Without feeling. Keeping the family name pristine and the accounts full—very fat and full—since before my 21st birthday." I scoffed, pushing around the last of the glazed chicken Micah had prepared earlier. "Little time to make or maintain friendships, because there's always a fire to put out. A deal to close. Which is why, and don't judge me..." I pointed at him. "I hired my private chef, who is in her sixties. She *feels* like a friend. She comes here to make food for me every so often and I love it— not because it's the best food I've ever tasted, but because she's an excellent passive listener. And sometimes I just need someone to listen and forget what I've told them, even if I have to pay them to do it." I smiled. "And she gives the best advice. No amount of money is enough for the advice she gives."

I lifted my gaze to Micah to see him quiet, completely focused in on me.

He asked, "And who takes care of you after you take care of everybody else?"

"Who takes care of you after you're done caring for your father?"

"Answer my question first."

No one was the answer I gave internally. Absolutely no-one.

The words would never leave my lips. The idea of someone taking care of me the way I took care of others was foreign. I wasn't sure I'd even know what to do with such care.

When I gave him no answer, a smile gradually pulled at Micah's lips.

"*Mmm-hmm,*" he teased. "That's *exactly* why the drink had to be called Control Issues and nothing else."

I rolled my eyes playfully, and he chuckled lowly.

"I can't help but wonder what you're like when you lose that control."

"Careful." I smirked, softly. "You might not survive me losing control, Micah."

He blew air through his lips and laughed—almost making me laugh too.

We finished the rest of our meal quietly, Micah immediately

getting to cleaning up, even though I told him I'd have cleaners here in the morning who could handle it.

But he insisted, and I watched him, in awe of a person who was so amazing in his own right.

I sat silently and he worked just as quietly, and the whole thing just felt like a sad goodbye.

I didn't like it.

Didn't feel right saying anything about it either.

He was only here to cook, and now he was done.

After he rinsed the final dish, I walked with him down the dimly lit hallway en route to the elevator.

The first time he was here, I noticed how the penthouse I'd been calling home for the past year felt different. Better. Thought it was all in my head until he arrived again tonight. And that feeling in my penthouse, of ease, calm, was back. But as we closed the distance between ourselves and the elevator he'd take to leave, I could feel that ease and calm dissipating.

"Another great meal," I said, turning to face him. "Thank you."

"You're welcome," he replied, voice easy. "Thanks for having me... again."

We stood there for a breath before he leaned forward to press the call button.

The door opened and I instantly felt my chest tighten. I glanced down the hall and into the living area of my penthouse.

Stillness. The cold glitter of neighboring high-rises. Emptiness.

All the things I've managed to deal with... but tonight, it just seemed too difficult to return to alone.

Micah somehow made the silence feel alive. Not heavy. While he cooked in my kitchen he made the air around me easier to breathe. He made my penthouse feel like home and for once, I didn't want to be alone in it.

"Good night, Ari." He smiled, immediately turning to step onto the elevator.

He stopped when I placed a hand on his arm.

Micah dropped his attention to where I held his arm, lifting his gaze to me next.

The air shifted.

What the hell was I doing?

I didn't know. I wasn't even sure if it was me... or something outside of me. But I couldn't let his arm go.

Let him go, Ari!

He glanced inside the elevator, then refocused on me.

I whispered, "I don't want you to go."

He held his gaze with me. "Why not?"

I've had to face some intimidating people in my life—people who were powerful enough to determine my fate in an industry that was male dominated—and I always did it fearlessly. But having to answer his question, *"Why not?"* was scary as hell.

Scary for what my answer would mean.

"Because... I feel sad. Juvenile as that sounds, it's true," I admitted. "I feel that way every night here, and I don't want to feel that way tonight."

With that—and with no hesitation—he stepped away from the elevator's entrance, the elevator door closing right after. Micah stepped closer to me, slowly, eyes never leaving mine.

Inches in front of me, he asked, "So, you want me to stay?"

I stared at him for a moment, then nodded.

He shook his head and took another step closer. I could feel the heat radiating off him, making my breaths harder to take.

"A nod isn't enough, it isn't words," he stated. "I *need* to *hear* you tell me to stay, Ari."

I didn't understand what I was feeling, only that it felt better than any other thing I've ever experienced in my life. Do you know how perplexing that can be to a woman like me? To be this person everyone believed had everything, *knew everything*, but to *never* have experienced whatever it was I was experiencing with Micah in that moment?

There was no way I could let him or *that* go.

Any reserve left in me that night was gone—entirely—when I obeyed and whispered, "Stay, Micah"

He cradled my face in his hands, then crashed his lips into mine.

The kiss was slow, gentle—like we were still questioning each other. Questioning this.

He guided me back against the elevator door, and with a surface to hold us up, we deepened our kiss.

I fisted his shirt, pulling him closer, tasting hints of our meal on his tongue, hearing him exhale a gratifying moan against me, melting me on impact.

The kiss went from questioning to knowing—intensifying, his hands everywhere on me... and me wanting more. Wanting him to go further. Deeper.

He moved his lips off mine and onto my neck, breathing heavily against me as he guided the thin skin into his mouth, drawing out a deep moan from me.

That control he wanted to see me lose was happening.

And his restraint was slipping.

Because all it took was that moan for him to lift me into his arms like I weighed nothing and to move us away from the elevator.

He didn't bother asking me where the bedroom was.

He just... *knew*.

The moment we crossed the threshold, everything just seemed to slow down in the best way.

Clothing was gone, trails of it created on my bedroom floor, leading to my bed.

What was left was the two of us, on my mattress—naked, not just physically, but in the ways that really counted.

"Tell me what your body needs right now."

His eyes, his skin, his body—they all looked so picturesque on my California King with the backdrop of lower Manhattan over his shoulder.

With the sights of New York City sparkling on the other side of my windows, providing the only light we needed, Micah was a vision I couldn't take my eyes off.

He smoothed his hands over my bare shoulder, gliding his fingertip down my chest, stopping at my nipple, where he brushed his thumb over the tip, making me arch my back under his control.

His fingertips continued mapping my skin, lowering to my abs, then my thighs, sending my temperature higher than before.

"Right about now... it needs everything," I whispered.

He smiled, leaned his body weight forward and onto me, encouraging me to lean back in bed.

He planted his arms on either side of me, balanced on his hands, and looked down at me.

"That's a lot of control you're forfeiting."

"It is, but something tells me you can handle it. "

We held the moment in silence before I lifted my hand and smoothed it down his chest.

"Make *me* a drink... literally." I quirked a smile, and he grinned in response.

"Do to me what you think I'd like," I started. "Then make me forget who I am... and learn who *you* are."

He held his stare with me, lowering slowly, pressing his mouth to mine, parting my lips with his.

And in that moment, his mouth tasted like safety... and everything but sadness.

He sheathed his erection with a condom but didn't guide himself inside me just yet.

Micah kissed his way down to my thighs, parting them to slide lower, teasing me with slow, calculated strokes of his tongue where I ached most.

And I unraveled completely. My voice traveled around us, his hands busy, caressing and kneading. He created tight tiny circles with his tongue in an unhurried rhythm. He tongued the spot that made me tremble, slow at first, then deeper until my hips couldn't stay still. I fisted the silk sheets and he closed his hands over my hands, sucking my clit between his thick lips until my back was curving off the mattress as a release rolled through me in a satisfying brief wave.

The same way he kissed his way down was the same journey his lips took back up to mine, guiding himself inside me once he reached eye level with me.

I gasped his entire way in, hands holding onto the wings of his back as he wound his hips while rocking in and out.

His skin against mine didn't feel like lust—it felt like something I'd never had: *relief*.

A release before it even began.

A rush of warmth that felt like it would be there forever, as if time meant nothing.

Nothing outside of what was happening on that bed mattered.

Like our only priority was his lips on my lips, his chest to mine, our bodies connected by slow friction, quivers, and measured deep strokes.

He wondered what it was like to see me lose control... and he got the best view.

And I didn't have any qualms about it.

I *wanted* him to see me.

I wanted to be heard by him.

This man—who was thirteen years my junior—wanted to understand me in ways no one had ever even tried to.

I turned over with him, our connection unbroken. His hands cupped my breasts as if he were memorizing me, each glide of my hips feeding something deeper... pleasure, need, a surrender I didn't want to stop. Micah traced fire with his fingertips against my skin. Used his hips to meet the twisting of my hips, his hard exhales mimicking his thrusts.

"Yes," I moaned, biting down on my lip, my head bowing forward. "Right there... don't stop."

Each slow circle of my waist and upstroke he delivered made me feel like I was dissolving into him.

The space around us was filled with a chorus of moans, groans, and whispered commands... most of them from him.

Soft claps of dewy bodies and unleashed emotions until he changed positions.

I was flat on the bed again, face buried in my pillows this time, him behind me, fingertips dug deep in my flesh when he turned my face by my jaw so he could kiss me from behind.

He remained still behind me, pausing any movements except the thrusts of his tongue against mine.

His knees caged me in.

I felt so full of him, so turned on even with him still as we kissed, that I couldn't resist doing the movements, working him in and out with only my hips.

I drove him in deep... then deeper.

He groaned each time I took him. One hand branded heat along my skin, the other held me in place as I used him to get myself off.

And Micah let me... he made himself my toy. He held himself statue-still, his erection stiff and heavy, his exhales syncing with my pace as I glided his dick in and out of me on my knees.

He released a guttural groan when my walls clenched tight around him, refusing to let go. Because I couldn't hold it back... I was coming.

"Damn, Ari... you're gonna wreck me like this, beautiful. My God."

A whimper escaped before I could stop it, the flutter of my walls so sharp I barely recognized the sound as mine.

He kissed the side of my mouth. "And I'll let you leave me with nothing when you feel this good full of me. Go 'head and take me apart. Take what you need."

I kept at it, until I worked myself to the point of trembling, losing my rhythm, my breath, and totally wrecking the flow.

I collapsed and was quivering around his shaft, my face buried in my pillow, breathless, when he asked in my ear, "Is it my turn again?"

He left a kiss there and didn't wait for me to answer before he was rocking into me now, taking over—resuming his strokes, like he never stopped, not missing a beat.

"You rode me like you needed every second." He turned my head to expose my lips to his and kissed me hard. "Now I gotta show you what it did to me."

I fisted the sheets when the fluttering inside me grew stronger —too strong to control. And it was happening so soon after the last release.

"Mmm, are you coming for me again, Ari?" He moaned against my neck, shuddering.

"Oooh, Micah." I gritted my teeth then anchored my head back. "Oh, God."

His hand now at my jaw held me steady, while the other at my waist guided me in slow, measured glides... control I should've resisted, but didn't want to.

"Is that a yes?" He peered down at me from behind with low lids and nodded.

"You coming, huh?" His voice dropped lower. "Good. 'Cause you deserve at least one more of those... and a whole lot more if I get my way."

Our bodies colliding created a rhythm I got lost in, sensitivity growing with each stroke from him, my head lighter, weightless. I dropped it forward to brace myself.

"There she go," he said, his voice trembling. "I'm with you."

I exhaled a broken sound.

"Oh, fuck." He groaned over my moaning, body quivering now. "I'm with you."

And what he believed I deserved hit me so suddenly and so hard, like a storm I didn't see coming.

A storm I didn't know he was referring to until I was caught in the eye of it.

Shaking, jaw slacked, and unable to breathe through it, control it.

It consumed me from my hair follicles to my toes, curling them.

I tried to hang on but couldn't.

Attempted to hold back, but there was no use.

So I surrendered and got swept away with him—losing myself in the rhythm of his hips, his groans rising with mine, like we were letting go in unison.

There was no bed where I was.

No air. No problems to fix.

Just Micah and me.

Before all of this, I thought I'd lose control with this man and instantly want it back.

But as his mouth found mine again from behind, and I inhaled his exhale—struggling, blissfully, to catch my breath, all I felt was... *free*.

Day 15: Lose Your Nerve

MICAH

I could hear her shuffling around in my sleep.

Feet padding lightly against hardwood, then clothing sliding over skin in a hurry.

I wasn't sure which of it made me blink awake.

The view of the Manhattan skyline was my first reminder I wasn't in my bed in Brooklyn. The second reminder came softer... silk sheets against my skin, too fine to be mine.

Then it was catching Arielle's shadow in my peripheral as it moved swiftly through her room.

I inhaled a deep breath and dragged a hand down my face.

"Hey," I rasped, pushing myself up and into a seat.

She stopped.

It almost appeared like she'd stopped breathing too.

Me noticing that caused my shoulders to slump a little.

She started walking again, moving faster about her room, but her eyes flicked toward me once.

Not cold. Not cruel.

Just afraid of staying still.

"I'm heading into *The St. James*," she uttered low, pulling her camisole over her head.

I turned to her night table, reaching for my phone and pressing the side button.

3:57 a.m.

It was three in the morning.

Way too early.

Way too obvious what this really was.

Before I could say any of that, Arielle disappeared inside a room near her bathroom.

I sighed, kicking my legs off the bed to stand up.

Grabbed my boxers that lay on the floor, stepped into them, and swaggered to the room she entered.

Her bedroom resembled a hotel, much like the rest of her place.

Luxurious. Rich. Spacious.

With everything in its place.

I didn't think past the sex.

Was shocked she let it happen—shocked she'd even asked me to stay when I was leaving.

I went with the flow, because life has taught me it's the best thing.

But this wasn't feeling right.

I stopped at the room's doorway and realized it was a walk-in closet.

Not your ordinary walk-in, though.

It resembled a boutique.

Clothing on opposite walls.

Shoes in clear cases.

In the middle of it all, a chaise and dresser with a marble counter.

Arielle stood on one end, sliding suits on hangers down the sparkling gold rods.

"You know it's three in the morning?" I asked her.

She paused when she heard my voice.

Inhaled a sharp breath next.

Then resumed sorting through the clothes.

I walked up to her, not stopping until I wrapped my arms around her waist from behind.

Last night was beyond what my imagination could've created about this woman.

I witnessed a side of her I knew others hadn't—and probably never would.

I doubted *I'd* ever again.

Still, I wrapped my arms around her and pulled her back gently against me.

No one would know how warm her body was.

How soft.

How vulnerable she could get.

"Last night..." she said low. "What we did..." She stated breathing harder. "As *amazing* as it was, *you* work for *me*, and you're *only* twenty-eight. And I'm... *shit*, I'm—"

"*Shh*" I shushed in her ear. "Relax, Ari. Just chill for me."

She shook her head. "Micah—"

"You don't have to run," I continued behind her. "Or explain, aight? Because I'm *not* asking for *anything* but *this* moment. Aight?"

She inhaled against me, and with her exhale, she relaxed a bit more.

Breathing steady.

Barely.

I could feel the tension fighting it.

Fighting the ease that could've been there between us.

I closed the distance between myself and the back of her neck.

Left a kiss there, allowing my lips to linger, knowing the privilege of being so close and understanding how temporary that was.

"Go back to bed," I said against her.

Gave her a kiss on her shoulder.

Then her cheek.

Wrapped my arm even tighter around her for one last embrace.

I stepped back, releasing her, turning to leave the walk-in. Never looking back.

Grabbed my clothes off the floor, stepped into my pants, slid on my shirt... all of it happening as I took steps toward her elevator.

I left, saying nothing else.

Made no sense to press.

It happened.

Last night happened.

I never thought past that.

Never thought of it in the first place.

But damn, dare to dream, right?

I was in my Range Rover, out of Manhattan and in Crown Heights in Brooklyn in under an hour.

Watched as the first light of morning cut through my windshield.

It was still too early for my shift at *The St. James*.

I wasn't due there until noon.

But it was too late to return to bed, too.

So when I got inside the apartment I shared with my father, I showered, freshened up, got dressed, and entered his bedroom.

When Arielle asked me to return to her penthouse to cook for her, I made arrangements with Ms. Thea.

She stayed the night, and was likely still asleep in the third available room in our pre-war apartment.

I knew she'd be up soon, though.

So I decided to spend the time in my dad's room.

The hums of his hospital bed and oxygen tank filled the sound space.

I walked up to him, watching his chest rise and fall, eyes closed. Rubbed lavender oil into his temples, hoping it eased him some. Then I reached for the tray of amber bottles, drew up the morphine, and let a few drops slip under his tongue. His jaw moved, just barely.

My dad was strong. Always had been. Seeing him like this—half the man he used to be—put a squeeze on my heart that hurt bad.

I sank into the chair by his bed, my usual spot, and leaned back, staring at the ceiling.

"Today," I said to it. "In the shower. I was thinking about that science project I did in third grade."

I lowered my chin to focus on my father.

"Everybody else decided their project would be a volcano, and I wanted something different. Something *more*. So, I did the light-bulb thing."

I smiled, then laughed a little.

"You called me a damn showoff." I laughed again, louder this time. "Said, 'Boy, you just always gotta aim higher than everybody else, just because.'"

I nodded. "Ain't nothing changed, Dad."

I scoffed, leaning forward to press my head into my hands.

"Her name's Arielle," I said, rubbing my hands down my face. "A St. James. Rich-ass family, man. I spent the night at her crib... a penthouse. Skyscrapers so close it felt unreal. Like the whole New York City skyline was sitting in a snow globe, just for her."

I licked my lips, then inhaled the air, picking up on the lavender I'd rubbed on him and the antiseptic that had been in the air for so many months I was sure it had become one with the walls.

"I spent the night at her home, in her world," I continued. "I liked her, but I didn't like *it*. Her home felt cold, like her at times. But when she let herself just be? She was warm. Soft. Softer than I ever expected. Like she was waiting for someone to make room for that side of her."

I'll never forget what she sounded like or how she looked with me inside of her. Never.

Her walls clenched around my dick, and I bit my bottom lip so hard holding back, I could taste blood. But I didn't care. I was buried deep in the most beautiful, the most amazing woman I'd ever known—and her moans were a battery in my back powering me through her pleasure, the only sound my ears would allow me to hear.

"Micah," she exhaled, tipping her head back against her pillow, the view of her slender neck at that angle making me harder. "Oh God, Micah."

I'd given her no reprieve. After she came the second time, I was right back on her. Only allowing her to catch her breath as I changed into the only other condom I had left in my wallet. The bite of sensitivity when I slid back inside her, so soon after coming with her, didn't matter to me. The pain, mixed with pleasure, was worth hearing her whisper my name like a prayer.

I went as deep as her body would allow, held onto every breath that would allow me to last inside her. I had no idea when I would ever have this opportunity again. So I wanted to make it last as long as possible.

And when I came, she came too—and the shit felt unreal. Euphoric. It was the second time tonight we wrecked each other at the same time. The first time felt like coincidence. But the way her walls clenched and released around my dick felt more in sync than anything I'd ever known.

My jaw was tight. Back aching. Dick throbbing.

Then Arielle took my face in her hands, made me watch, made me feel my nut climb to an unbearable high. Her moans ricocheted off the walls, matching mine. Everything hit a breaking point. A chill ran through me, settling at the base of my spine.

One look at Arielle—and her looking at me—had me losing it inside of her... and her losing it with me again.

And when we finally let go, the eruption left me with nothing left to hold onto. No strength. No fight. Just me collapsing against her, breathless.

Right before I left her penthouse, I told her I only wanted the moment. Meant it, too... at the time. But now, with thoughts of last night on my mind, the taste of her I swore I could still savor on my tongue, I wanted more. And that was a problem.

"She's 41." I couldn't help but smile. "She won't say it out loud, but I already know. Found her wiki page after my first day working at her hotel. *Her* hotel, man. Shorty owns a whole luxury hotel, Dad. She a boss. The *baddest* I've ever seen, let me tell you."

I nodded, leaning my head back against the neck of the chair again.

"You always said I never took the easy way." I smiled. "And I guess I never really learned how. Because it would be me to go for the boss, knowing I'm *way* outta my league, but aiming that high anyway. Shit."

I leveled my head to see my father's head turned in my direction, eyes open.

I sat up immediately.

There was a flicker of recognition in his eyes, and that made me stutter an inhale.

I stood from my seat, made my way to him, feeling my chest grow tight as soon as I was by his side.

Took his hand, and he weakly closed his hand around mine.

I pressed my free hand to his forehead and smiled.

"Only took me telling you I was with a 41-year-old heiress for you to open them eyes, huh?" My smile grew bigger. "You always did like eavesdropping on gossip."

"Good morning," Ms. Thea greeted to my left.

"Yes, it is." I nodded, squeezing my dad's hand a little more. "A *very* good morning."

I spent another hour in my dad's room.

Ms. Thea doing her thing. Massaging his hands and feet. Gently wiping sweat away from his brows with a cool cloth.

She and I joked, laughed, my dad's eyes following it all.

He didn't say anything—knew he wouldn't, since he hasn't said much at this stage—but he was cognizant.

Present.

And that was enough.

It was time for me to head out when I leaned forward, kissed his forehead, and told him, "Hold it down 'til I get back, King."

An hour later, I was at *The St. James* for my shift. With an added pep in my step, despite arriving to see Arielle's office door closed again.

Since my days of drink deliveries, she's kept it open.

It was how I had my in.

By hour four of my shift, it was clear that her door was staying closed for the day.

Was she even here?

That afternoon at *The St. James* was not what I expected.

I didn't really expect much though.

I just knew she was in her head now... and I couldn't get there.

And maybe I was in mine too. Overthinking.

I'd *never* been with a woman like Arielle.

Older women had always been my thing. Maturity, confidence, no drama, just real talk and good energy. They knew who they were. That steadiness did something for me.

And in bed? Different story altogether. They owned their bodies. No proving, no pretending.

Just... pleasure.

Desire sat richer in them.

I grew up fast, so they noticed me before girls my age ever did. My first real relationship, I was twenty-three, she was thirty-eight. I got a kick out of being underestimated, then proving myself—in conversation, at work, in bed.

Women my age? Still figuring it out. Nothing wrong with that. Just not for me. I wanted someone sure. Someone steady.

And Arielle checked every box. Older, confident, sharp as hell. But she also knocked me sideways. Made me restless. Doubtful. Like no matter how much I proved, I still wanted to prove more. No other woman ever had me like that. It was frustrating as hell. And addicting as fuck.

By hour five, I was behind the bar, mixing drinks, carrying on conversations with the rooftop crowd like always, but it was all a blur.

A spring of hope arrived when I spotted Arielle through the rooftop's glass door.

She was passing through, accompanied by Charmaine, her assistant, but Arielle didn't peer through the glass once at me.

It was like seeing a ghost.

I was numb after that.

Talked myself into believing it was fine.

She was protecting herself. She had every right to. I get it.

But damn... I couldn't talk myself out of the hollow in my chest or the weight sitting heavy in my gut.

No communication whatsoever?

More closed off than before?

It wasn't looking good.

Near the end of my shift, the second bartender arrived.

As I gathered my things, I realized I'd missed a couple of recent calls from Ms. Thea.

I was unlocking my phone to call her back when she called again.

I answered on the first ring.

"Mic," she said low, and my heart dropped.

Her tone was different.

But not different enough for me not to pick up on the reason.

"Mic... his breathing's changed, baby," she told me. "Shallow. Slow."

"Aight..." I forced out.

"He's cold to the touch," she whispered. "Eyes haven't opened in hours since you left."

I inhaled a staggered breath, swallowing hard.

"I think it's time, Micah."

Nothing else mattered in that moment.

I grabbed my stuff, told the bartender to step in for me a little earlier than usual, which they were cool with.

I didn't even bother clocking out. I just... left.

Hopped in my Range Rover, drove on high speed, taking a few red lights until I was outside my apartment building in Brooklyn, parking and bursting through the lobby door and jogging up the stairs.

I sprinted through the front door, my breath caught in my chest.

Ms. Thea waited for me at the end of the apartment's hallway, near his room.

She guided me into a hug when I was close, and for a moment, I felt like I was outside of myself.

We knew the day would come, but still... this didn't feel real.

It almost felt shocking.

"Am I too late?"

"No, he waited for you," she said in my ear before letting me go so I could enter his bedroom.

His chest wasn't rising and falling smoothly like that morning.

The hum of the machine was more like a dragging of air, as he visibly struggled to pull it in.

My bottom lip was quivering as I pulled the chair I'd been sitting in for months—every morning — closer to his bedside.

I took my seat and took his cold hand.

I sucked my teeth, dropped my forehead against it, and didn't fight back the choking urge to cry.

This shit hurt. Damn.

Tears welled in my eyes, the weight of it all sitting on my chest and my shoulders.

His breathing became shallower, like he was forcing in the air now.

"It's aight."

I kissed his hand and left my mouth there.

"You did good. You did *so* good. I'm beyond proud of you. You sure showed that doctor he didn't know what he was talking about, right? 'Cause you got heart, man. To the very end, you had heart."

I squeezed his hand, lifting it to kiss it twice.

"Thank you, Dad. Thank you. For it all."

I lifted my eyes to his closed ones, the tears streaming. "You can rest now. Rest, King."

A few seconds later, he inhaled one long, deep breath... and then settled.

His final.

Soon, the room was quiet.

His chest still.

I could feel Ms. Thea in the room with me, but she remained quiet, too. Respectful, as always.

I ran my thumb along my father's still hand, leaning forward one more time to press a kiss to it.

"You waited for me," I acknowledged. "You held it down, just like I asked. Thank you."

Day 21: Lose Your Anchor

ARIELLE

I ran my fingers through my hair, making a mental note to have Charmaine set up a hair appointment. My roots were starting to curl again. I needed to get them straightened.

My mother used to love my curls when I was little. I did too. But after her death and as I took on more of the family business, I've chosen to keep them tamed. Straight. Controlled.

It made life feel easier without having to manage the maintenance of curls.

I rolled my leather desk chair closer to my desk. It was cluttered with folders, papers, and sticky notes. Laptop screen open to the updated *St. James Table* renovation proposal.

With a pen in hand, I started marking up versions of Micah's recent cocktail menu additions, my mind constantly escaping the task and drifting back to last week.

Six days.

It had been six days since we'd last spoken, seen each other.

I shook my head to refocus.

The way I had been working these past few days was reminiscent of the days when Julian and I were brainstorming the launch of *The St. James* in New York.

Mostly me.

Julian was busy shopping and getting fittings for the launch party.

My point was that I was inundating myself in *The St. James Table* business as if I was trying to get something off the ground... when really, I'd been trying to get my senses in order.

Micah and I had sex.

I had him in places in me I didn't think anyone could ever reach. Physically, emotionally, mentally.

I could still smell him on my silk bed sheets. His cologne or body oil, I couldn't tell. Cedarwood and smoked vanilla. Clove? I don't know.

Whatever it was, its subtle warmth lingered on my damn pillowcases. Long after the cleaning lady put it through several cycles, I could still smell him. Every night since.

And it didn't help with me missing him.

Which was insane, right?

I missed him.

Had only known the man for 21 days, slept with him after knowing him for 14... and I was already missing him.

I shook my head harder this time, lifting the cocktail menu closer to my eyes.

It didn't help that what I was marking up involved him.

I had been *so* over-involved these past few days—reviewing costs, labor timelines, and ingredient sourcing.

I hadn't done stuff like this since... the start of all *this*. Normally, tasks like this would be delegated to my bar manager or the finance team.

But I needed the distraction. I needed to keep my brain busy, because left on its own, it would keep bombarding me with memories of the night I slept with Micah.

The night he made me feel like the woman I've always wanted to be.

The night he made me forget who I was—and learned who *he* was.

A man, not a boy in the least, filled with fire and soul, with a calm beneath all that heat.

He was late-night jazz and easy laughter.

That night, his hands moved with purpose, exploring every inch, curve, flaw.

God... I could still feel him and he was nowhere near me.

I ran my fingertips across my neck where he'd kissed me so many times I could still feel his lips there.

I bit at my bottom lip and crossed my legs beneath my desk, trying to calm the ache starting between my thighs, caused by just the memory of us in my bed.

Avoiding him was necessary because of *this*.

Going through withdrawal from something I'd only experienced once.

I've replayed our night together more times than I'll *ever* allow myself to admit.

Even after the sex, he was still so affectionate. Kissing my shoulder randomly when he thought I was asleep.

With Julian, it was sex. Quick. Empty. Forgettable.

With Micah, it was lovemaking that wrapped around me, before, during, and even after the act... like his presence never left my body.

What the hell had I gotten myself into?

He hadn't brought any drinks to my desk since that night.

Hadn't knocked on my closed office door.

I could've left it open, but I was conflicted.

So conflicted.

He'd left his shift earlier than usual the night after we slept together and had changed shifts with our other bartender without permission a day after that. I let it be. Avoiding interaction.

I'd convinced myself that the distance I'd created between us was for the best.

It was just *one* night.

He was young.

We were nothing more than a moment.

That's *all* we could ever be.

But shit, I couldn't help but feel like that moment was becoming something I'd lost and not something I'd actually had.

There was a sharp knock at my door that pulled me back behind my desk.

"Come in, Charmaine," I said, lowering my attention to the paperwork again.

I looked up as the door opened to find Micah standing at the doorway.

My brows relaxed—and so did I—as I leaned back in my chair.

He was dressed casually in his usual black slim-fit dress shirt, rolled up sleeves, matching slacks, and designer sneakers. Simple, still sexy, and not helping with me recalling how much of an Adonis he is with nothing on.

Something was different though, about him. His eyes... redder. Posture guarded. Civil.

He usually leaned on my doorframe with a certain familiarity.

In the days after we slept together, when I wasn't forcing myself not to think of him, some days fantasies would push through.

One of me waiting for him to show up at my office. To casually stand at my door, look at me with those dreamy eyes of his and that mischievous grin and say, *"Tonight I'm coming over again. And after, let's not act like what we do didn't happen."*

But today, he didn't arrive that version of himself at all.

Today, his hands were in his pockets. Shoulders squared.

I straightened in my seat at that. Relaxed the tension in my jaw.

I said nothing.

He didn't either. For a little.

Until...

"I just wanted to come in and give notice."

I blinked hard.

"I know you said during my interview how you guys change bartenders a lot around here, and I hate to do it but..."

He folded his bottom lip into his mouth, dragging his top teeth over it. His habit I found unbelievably sexy. Even more now.

"I'll be leaving *The St. James.*"

My heart tanked. It literally felt like it dropped to the pit of my stomach.

I blinked harder than before, my jaw slacking a little, my mouth going dry.

I formed my lips to question the first time, but I couldn't get anything out.

I swallowed, inhaled a breath to regain my poise. My mask?

"What?"

It's the one word I could actually get out, and he didn't respond.

I ran my fingers through my hair, moving the strands off my shoulder. "Is this about... what happened?"

What I really wanted to ask was... had I made the distance between us too wide?!

He shook his head. "Not at all."

I tried like hell to compose myself, but my heart was hammering.

I've dealt with bartenders quitting all the time, leaving with no notice at all, sometimes.

This should have been the same.

But it wasn't.

I *knew* this bartender in the biblical sense.

But beyond that, I *really* liked him here.

"Then... if it's not because of what happened—"

"My father passed."

I couldn't stop the gasp if I tried. My hand flew to my mouth a second later.

I wanted to stand from my seat, go to him, but I anchored myself where I was.

The door was open, people were within earshot.

I. Can't.

"Oh, my God," I expressed lowly. "Micah." I pressed my hand to my chest next. "When?"

"A few days ago," he replied, his Adam's apple bobbing as he pressed his lips into a thin line. "The evening... *after.*"

He didn't have to clarify when *the evening after* was. I know *exactly* what he's referring to—it was in the brief clench of his jaw.

"I'm so sorry," I whispered. "Why didn't you tell me sooner?"

He shrugged, eyes never leaving mine when he added, "What would you have done?"

The question sliced me right in the chest.

It seemed like a simple question but it hit me hard.

Because how could I ask him that when *I'd* been avoiding *him*?

I was doing the bar manager's work, for God's sake. All so I could avoid Micah.

I squeezed my eyes closed, briefly, reopening them and not feeling any better after.

"Anyway, *uh*..." He ran a hand from the top of his head down his mouth. Gestured behind himself with his thumb. "I booked a one-way ticket to Paris."

The air thinned.

"Oh," I expressed.

He released a scoffing laugh, but the smile I've always loved seeing on his face returned... briefly.

"I don't know where I'm gonna stay but..."

He rubbed his lips together.

"My father had a million-dollar insurance policy in his name before he got sick. He's left everything to me. He's gone, and Paris is there. The cuisine program at Le Cordon Bleu starts in June and runs until December. I figured I'd just hop on the plane, figure everything out when I get there in time to be ready for June."

I nodded slowly.

I felt weighted in my seat, my heart a ton heavier.

I was running my tongue along my teeth behind my lips, trying like hell not to show the panic climbing up my throat—because why the hell *was* I panicking?

We spoke about this. His dreams, aspirations. This made sense. Him going made sense.

I wasn't thinking about having to interview another bartender, start the process all over again.

My mind was squarely on *him leaving... for good. For better.*

I lifted my eyes to see him staring at me. His eyes darted between mine, saying nothing—but everything too.

Like that night, his eyes barely ever left mine. Watching me as his fingertips sketched heat on my body. His attention fixed on me as my eyes blurred from coming so hard my vision became clouded with tears.

"There's nothing keeping me here anymore..." He blinked but didn't break eye contact when he added, "Right?"

Here I was again with *all* the power.

Like always.

The power to decide how something moved, what it became. All the shit I never asked for.

Because I didn't ask for *this*.

This challenge. This whisper of possibility.

I stared back at him, parting my lips then quickly closing them when nothing came out.

Because I could tell him to stay.

Tell him he could work in *The St. James Table's* kitchen.

He did a fantastic job as a fill-in.

Patrons were still raving about that night and the food Micah prepared—something our head chef, André, finds both intriguing and offensive.

I parted my lips to say that, to lead with the suggestion and the offer, but I closed my mouth. Rubbed my lips together and swallowed the words like medicine I didn't want but knew I needed.

I could've just told Micah to stay, just like I did that night...

But I didn't.

"Right," I voiced. "There's nothing keeping you here. Paris makes sense."

His shoulders sag, the fight leaving him.

And I wanted to take it back. But the words had already landed. Too calm. Too fucking final.

"Paris is the right move for you, Micah," I said, this time with more conviction. "It's the right thing to do. You're so young. Brilliant. With the proper training, and with the prestige and experience of Le Cordon, you're going to be *amazing*. Unstoppable by the time you get to my age."

I released a laugh, hoping to soften the moment. To soften *myself*.

Because Lord knows as much as my mouth was saying those words, my heart was *not* in agreement.

It was beating so hard it was as if it were trying to beat its way out of my chest, to run into his arms. Beg him to take me with him... away from here.

Take me with him, *wherever* in Paris he was going. I didn't care...

Just take me with you.

How ridiculous was that? Right?!

Micah nodded, visibly not offended. But it was like my words knocked the smile out of his eyes. Made him close himself off a little from me.

A second later, he dipped his head toward me and simply turned on his sneakers, leaving as quietly as he'd entered.

He didn't look back.

Didn't offer a *see you later* or an indication that he'd be back before he actually went.

He just kept walking, his silhouette fading like smoke.

And that's how I knew he wasn't coming back.

His quiet exit left me at my desk... unsure.

Empty again.

An emptiness I hadn't felt since I walked into *Vesper* and saw him standing behind the bar, waiting to be interviewed by me.

Twenty-one days of knowing him felt like a new lifetime.

And just like that... it was over.

I inhaled a deep breath and let it out of my mouth, feeling my heart ache even more, gaining none of the relief I hoped.

My office was quiet again.

As if he'd never stepped through its door.

Micah hadn't been in my life long enough to tie me down. But for the first time in my life... I *wanted* an anchor.

I relaxed my shoulders, straightened my back, and pushed aside the folder that held a spreadsheet, forcing myself to redirect my focus.

I picked up the mocktail menu I'd been working on before Micah stepped into my office.

The menu he helped me sketch after he made the first drink for me after he began working at the St. James.

Control Issues.

His notes were still in the margin.

I closed my eyes, squeezing them shut as I pushed out all the air inside me through my mouth.

I pressed the menu to my chest next and dropped my head to it, feeling the tears build behind my eyes.

"Why didn't you just *say* something?" I whispered.

And I wasn't sure if I was asking me, or him.

Us both?

Because I just watched the one man who's ever made me feel like my worth was more about *who I was* and less about *what I did* walk out of my door... and my life...

And I didn't stop him.

I didn't let my guard down.

Didn't release control.

I didn't tell him to stay.

And for the first time in my life, I wanted to lose the control I've always been proud of having over myself.

I wanted nothing to do with it.

I wanted it gone.

Day 34: Lose Your Mask

ARIELLE

"Thank you," I said to my chauffeur, who held the backseat door open for me to step out of the car. My heels met the concrete and clicked beneath me as I closed the distance between myself and the turnstile doors of my father's high-rise building.

The night before, I enjoyed the best sleep I'd had in days—mostly because of what I planned to do today.

I nodded toward security, the gentleman greeting me with a smile as I walked to the bank of elevators. Today was a day in the making. The start of my new life. And I was eager to get it over with.

And to think, it all started with a private soul food dinner in my kitchen the week prior.

My private chef, Gloria Whitaker—who I, and everyone she knows, calls Glo—moved around my kitchen like she owned it... because technically, she did.

The only other person to cook in it besides Micah. This kitchen was so much Gloria, that wherever the pots were in the cabinets, the spices in the pantry, she'd put them there—and I left them alone.

"You look sad, child," she said to me as she stirred her creamy mac and cheese in the bowl. "Like really sad."

I snorted a laugh, leaning my chin into my hand. "Thanks, Glo."

"I'm serious, baby," she added, bending over just a little to spoon the mac and cheese into a casserole dish. "You look the most down I've ever seen you."

I sighed, closing my eyes a little. "Glo, do you remember that recipe I gave you a few weeks ago?"

She turned to glance at me, then refocused on her work. "I do. The short ribs."

I nodded. "The guy who gave it to me... he left the country."

She blinked in response. "And judging by how much sadder you just got, I'm guessing y'all had a thing."

"A very little thing," I confirmed. The aroma of the fried chicken she'd plated and sat in front of me was calling my name. I couldn't wait to dig in once she was done with the rest of the food.

I met Gloria while I was at a gourmet market, not far from my hotel, picking up sparkling water. She was having a random conversation with a cashier about a restaurant she once owned in Brooklyn, off Fulton Street in Bed-Stuy, where she was born and raised. Her energy was familiar, as weird as that might sound. So familiar I asked if she cooked privately for clients. She told me she didn't. So I asked if she'd like to, and she'd been cooking for me ever since I moved into the penthouse.

"And as little of a thing as he and I had," I continued, "I haven't felt like myself since he left and I don't understand why."

She smiled to herself. "Love will do that to you."

"Love is a stretch, Glo."

"A very real stretch." She laughed. "That thang will catch you when you least expect it, too. Don't matter how long you've known the person—"

"Or how old they are?"

She stopped what she was doing, placing the spoon down on the counter.

"He's 28."

She smirked knowingly. "And how old are you again?"

"41."

She whistled, then giggled. "Oh, now I know that thang y'all had wasn't little at all, baby."

I released a scoffing laugh, dropping my head into my hands.

Glo made it really easy to open up to her. So comforting, nonjudgmental—but also no-nonsense too. She reminded me a lot of my mom, and that was one of the reasons I hired her to come to my home and cook every once in a while.

"So is that why he left?" she asked. "Why you look so sad?"

"He lost his dad... and bought a one-way ticket to France."

"Aww, okay."

"I guess..." I started, "I never imagined him being at the hotel for long, bartending. But I also didn't think he'd be there for that short of a time."

"I mean, did you tell him to stay, at least?"

"I didn't." I shook my head. "He's young, brilliant, extremely talented. Asking him to stay would have been selfish."

Glo blinked in response.

"He makes me happy," I revealed, allowing myself to smile to myself. "And I didn't realize I wasn't happy until he made me feel what happy felt like."

Glo pressed her hand to her chest and smiled. "Arielle."

I closed my eyes and inhaled a deep breath. "He would have stayed if I asked him to. Deferred his dreams for me. And for what? Because he made me happy?"

I shook my head.

Happiness is a luxury, Glo. Not a priority."

"See, that's your problem right there, Arielle. You treat happiness like it's dessert... nice to have, but never on the menu. Maybe if you let yourself have a bite every now and then, you wouldn't look like you're starving for it."

I pursed my lips together and she laughed.

"So why not go to him?"

I jerked my head back.

"He's in France." She gestured with the stirring spoon in hand.

"Then go to France."

"I can't just go to France, Glo," I reasoned. "What would my family do without me? Everything would fall apart."

"I don't know. Maybe they'd figure it out?" She pressed her hand to her waist. "Finally start doing for themselves like they're supposed to?"

I stared at her for a moment and she held her stare with me.

I opened my mouth to say something in defense, but when the words formed—when I was just about to say, "No they won't, Glo" —I felt... silly.

Because why wouldn't they? My father was an established business man, Julian the same. They were able-bodied, intelligent men, thriving in an industry that praised intelligence in men and punished it in women. If they had no choice, no one to just drop everything on, wouldn't they just figure it out?

It was such a simple realization—maybe they'll figure it out— but it clung to me. I guess hearing someone else say it out loud helped me perceive it differently.

"You think the world will fall apart just 'cause you ain't the one holding it up?" She leaned an arm on the counter. "You think that makes you useful? Powerful? Being other people's crutch because you think they can't stand on their own when they're more than able to? Baby, that's not power. That's fear."

She took a pause.

"If the only thing holding you here is the worry of things falling apart without you being here... that sounds more like a death sentence you've given yourself." She tapped her chest lightly. "Death of self. Death of joy. The characteristics of the real walking dead. Might as well call yourself a zombie."

I moved my eyes off her, letting them drift around the kitchen, digesting her words.

"Sometimes, Arielle, love means dropping the reins, so your hands are free to hold something else."

I twisted my lips to one side.

"I'm thinking," she said, turning to open the oven door, "you didn't let that young man leave for his future. I think you pushed him out because you were afraid of yours."

That night, after Glo left and I was alone again—back in my bedroom, on my oversized King mattress—I sat with my back against the headboard, staring out at the glittering city skyline.

The penthouse felt loud in its silence. My heartbeat was in my ears as I shut my eyes, knowing sleep wouldn't find me.

Micah was everywhere, even though he wasn't here.

I reached for the pillow that still smelled like him. I'd asked my housekeeper to wash the silk bedding *again*. She did. His scent was fading. But not completely. It still lingered in the fibers.

So I pressed the pillow to my face and inhaled deeply, the ache in my chest flaring sharp. The night we spent together rushed in like a flood. No one had ever cared for me the way he did. Made me feel *so* good.

And I threw it away. Chose discipline over relief.

I willingly resisted—something Arielle St. James always did. And now I was here... sitting in the wreckage of everything I thought I had to hold onto.

The tears stung the backs of my eyes as I lowered the pillow from my face.

"Don't you cry right now," I whispered to myself, repeating what my father always said whenever I was faced with a challenge no young girl should've had to handle.

A deal falling through. A buyer walking. A proposal rejected.

"Your mother would fix this if she were here. So... just fix it," he'd say, with a wave of his hand and a sip of his drink. *"That's what she did and now that's what you do, Ari... you fix, kid. So, fix it."*

He was right. And so was Glo.

Today, I was going to do the final fixing. One that would work in my favor... for once.

Because I refused to be like the man in that book Micah was reading at *The St. James Table* bar.

I was done wondering how much longer I'd have to pretend fixing was all I was good for, just to survive.

The elevator doors opened to my father's private office. The space was all leather, glass, and ego. Awards displayed on every wall, his photo or name visible wherever the eyes landed.

My father, at his prime, was an industry genius. A legacy builder. A public icon. He made a lot of his money from our multi-generational business empire in luxury hospitality.

My mother, Robin St. James, was the backbone of the operation. A quietly powerful woman. Not flashy, not dominant. She was my father's mastermind alliance full of grace, wisdom, ad emotional intelligence. She was a schoolteacher before she became a philanthropist after marrying into the St. James family. Then she became my father's left arm with poise, patience, and an ability to command a room with a look, not volume. They were magic together. But she preferred to work behind the scenes of it all. My father was the face; he *loved* the attention.

Image was everything. And still was, for him.

When she passed, our home lost its warmth. And I stepped into her role. She was barely gone before people started saying, *"Well, Ari. I guess it's up to you now, huh?"*

I still remembered the night my father poured himself another glass of Scotch and waved me over to sit. It was a few days after we buried my mother, the triplex still smelled like her... at least I could still smell her perfume in the air. My father's eyes were glassy, but his voice steady.

"Your mother had it right, Ari," he told me, swirling the amber in his glass. *"I build it, I put the name on the door, I make the world look. But it's women like her... and now you... who keep the damn thing alive. You've got the head for it. The stomach. The touch.*

Men?" He smirked, tapped his chest. "We're good at starting wars. Women? You finish them. That's why this family still stands."

He clinked his glass against the arm of his chair, like it was a toast. "So don't look at me for the details. You're the details now. Just like your mother was. Make us proud, kid."

Quiet as kept, while her stroke played a role in her passing, the stress of running an empire with a man who was drunk most of the time, contributed to her death.

That wouldn't be *my* fate.

I greeted my father's assistant and pushed my way through his private office door.

He insisted that I meet with him here instead of at the triplex when I told him I needed to discuss *The St. James*. My father, Julian, and I were all in a partnership on the New York City location—the flagship.

The St. James brand had properties across the country—Chicago, South Beach, even one overseas in London. But this one, here in New York, was different. It was the *only* one I helped build from the ground up. The only one I worked on side-by-side with both my father and my ex-husband.

And I was done.

My father told me he had his girlfriend now calling the triplex home. Old me would have given him a spiel about that. Today, I didn't care.

I also didn't comment on the glass of Scotch he kept nearby at ten in the morning.

"Hey, Dad," I said as I stepped into his office.

"Ari." He nodded, leaning back in his chair. "What was so urgent it couldn't wait for an email?"

I reached his desk and placed the folder down in front of him.

"*The St. James*."

One brow ticked up. "What about it?"

"I'm offering you a clean transition."

His body shifted slightly, eyes narrowing. "A transition from what?"

"*The St. James* in New York," I said, crossing my legs as I sat. "My stake. My role. The 5 a.m. emails. The midnight calls. The damage control. The legacy."

"God." He scoffed. "Not *this* again. You had one bad quarter and now you're walking away?"

"Oh, this isn't about the bad quarter and I'm *not* walking away." I smiled. "I'm walking *forward*, Dad. With crystal-clear clarity. And with terms—because Daddy didn't raise a fool."

I slid the folder I placed on his desk closer to him. A folder I'd gathered at the biggest meeting of my career.

At that meeting, my pen hovered over the dotted lines. I couldn't help wondering: what if the board revolted? What if the press painted me as the St. James who broke the legacy instead of saving it? Julian would gloat. My father would sneer. I could already hear the whispers at galas—coward, quitter, weak link. But for once, I cared less about their whispers than I did about saving myself.

"Seventy-five percent of my equity. Clean transfer. You get majority control. I keep twenty-five percent for investment growth, and I'll retain the St. James name for select licensing opportunities."

He studied me from his seat. "And this decision was made when?"

"Last week," I answered. "Legal reviewed it. Board's been informed."

My father flashed a tight smile. "So you came here not to ask. You came here to announce."

"Precisely," I said. "Because, it's like I've said... Daddy didn't raise a fool."

I could've restructured, handed off pieces, reshuffled the deck chairs. But that would've been another prison... new walls, same cage. What I wanted wasn't a reshuffle. I wanted release. A clean break my father would *never* grant me, so I had to grant it to myself.

There was silence. Only the soft flush of the vents cycling fresh air into his pristine office with the city view.

"Is this about the bartender, Ari?"

I pressed my tongue to the roof of my mouth, making sure to take a breath.

"Julian said you'd been seeing him secretly." He chuckled. "Told me he quit on you guys not long ago and you've been moping around the hotel ever since."

I inhaled a reassuring breath, calming myself, knowing that I planned to deal with Julian's ass accordingly next.

When I decided to make this move—give up my stake in the New York City location while retaining only twenty-five percent to maintain a passive income—I knew I'd get pushback.

The donkey who thought she had built a legacy had actually built a stage for the ones around her to showboat.

But now it was time to stop performing.

"You would really give this up for a *man*, Ari? A 28-year-old at that?"

"I'm giving this up for myself," I said firmly. "*None* of you listen to me, and you hate me more and more for speaking reason into you. You all do whatever you want, and now you'll have the opportunity to do what you've always done—but this time in peace. And without a single word from me. I am *finally* done. I'm finished."

My father swallowed hard.

"And for the first time in my life... I'm *okay* not proving anything to you or *anyone* else. If you feel I'm giving this up for a man, fine. Think that. Think *whatever* you want. It doesn't change the fact that I'm wrapping this game up, and I'm taking my very *tired* ball home, Dad. You all can play amongst yourselves with your own big manly balls from here on out."

"Ari—"

"You told me years ago that men start wars and women finish them. Well, Dad, I'm finishing it. I'm done."

"You think this will last?"

I blinked.

"Ari, come on. You are business to the bone. I've raised you to be. You've got the Midas touch," he offered. "You fix. You make money. It's in your blood. It's your passion. And you *don't* quit your passion."

I scoffed.

"So, what? You're just going to live the rest of your days doing *nothing* in New York? Wasting your gifts?"

"I'm going to Paris."

"Paris?!" He laughed, his humor bouncing off the walls, echoing down the halls. "So this *is* about the damn bartender. Isn't *he* there?"

"Paris isn't about *him*, Dad. It's about me," I told him. "About finding something that isn't built on obligation or inheritance. Something *I* choose. And I choose *there*."

I stood from my seat and his eyes followed me.

"So that's *it*?"

"That's it," I replied. I made my way over to his side of the desk, leaned forward, and pressed a kiss to his cheek. Placed my hand on his shoulder and said, "I guess it's up to you now, kid. Make me proud."

He chuckled, shaking his head.

"See you around, Mr. St. James."

He was quiet as I made my way to his office door and opened it.

"For what it's worth," he said. "You did good, Ari. Your mother would've been proud."

I paused, forcing my attention to remain forward.

"*I'm* proud of you, kid."

I smiled to myself. "I know."

———

My next and final stop was *The St. James*. I stepped through the doors, eyes scanning the sophisticated minimalism. Everything about this place—from the curated art collection featuring Black artists from around the world to the scented hallways—was all me. Quiet luxury and exclusivity were the goal. And for what it *was* worth, I achieved that, and then some.

Now it was time to go. And right on time, because when I stepped through the doors, I couldn't ignore how dead it had become since Micah's been gone.

Wasn't here for long, but left not an impression but an imprint... on my heart.

I stopped at my office, finding Charmaine at her desk in front of it, doing what she always did on weekday mornings—be an amazing assistant.

"Ms. St. James," she said, standing from her seat. "I was wondering if you were going to make it in today."

"I'm only here for a short while." I smiled. "And so are *you*."

She wrinkled her brows.

"Charm, I'm letting you go."

She dropped back into her seat and parted her lips to say something, but stopped when I laid the check I'd already written out on her desk in front of her.

Her eyes grew as she surveyed the check, picking it up to bring it closer to her face.

"Oh my *God*, this is—"

"Three years' worth of your salary," I finished. "Exactly how much you would earn working for me as my assistant if you continued working for the next three years. Plus a few thousand extra."

She stared at me like I had three heads.

"You've spoken to me a couple of times about attending cosmetology school but not having enough to do that *and* keep a job." I gestured at the check. "*Now* you have everything you need to follow your dreams. So follow them."

She shook her head, jaw slacked, utterly speechless.

I pointed at her. "Promise me you'll make good on your

word. You'll go to school without worrying about money and you'll finish."

"I swear," she whispered, nodding. "I'll do that and more."

Charmaine's eyes welled with tears and I smiled, offering a nod, and turning to walk away.

"*Oh*, Ms. St. James," she called.

I turned back to her.

She was up on her feet, walking a sticky note over to me. She handed it to me, and my eyes read the words. A French address.

"Micah called this morning."

I fixed my eyes on hers.

"He told me to write down exactly what he spelled out and to give it to you the next time I saw you." She smiled. "This is the next, and well..." She laughed softly. "The *last* time I'm seeing you."

It was like he was reading my thoughts from thousands of miles away... and answering them without saying a word.

Like he'd reached across the ocean just to catch me thinking about him.

I folded the sticky note and dropped it into my bag.

"Thank you, Charmaine."

"Thank *you*, Ms. St. James." She nodded while smiling. "Thank you *so* much."

The walk to Julian's side of the hotel was brief. I barely made my way to that side of the hotel—wanting to have as little contact with my ex-husband as possible since our divorce. But today, I was making an exception. Because it would be my first and last time walking these floors.

Much like my father's office, Julian's corner office at *The St. James*—his, on the top floor—was all glass, leather, and excess.

What I didn't account for was his wife, Karmen, being present. I spotted her as soon as I approached his glass door.

His assistant peeked up from her computer and quickly slid her chair back on its wheels.

"No need to get up, Britney," I said, holding up a hand. "I won't be long."

Before she could say anything, I pushed open his door and noticed him smirking without looking up from the laptop he typed on.

"Is it time for the Birkin meeting?" he asked, tossing a look to Karmen.

I glanced over at Karmen to see her smiling cunningly before Julian was my focus again.

"I'm not here about the Birkin at all."

Julian looked up from his laptop.

"I'm here to tell you I'm leaving."

"Leaving... *what*?" he questioned. "A meeting? The hotel for home?"

I placed a folder—identical to the one I left with my father—on Julian's desk.

"I'm selling 75% of my stake in *The St. James, New York*," I announced. "The deal is nearly finalized."

His brows pulled in, his smirk fell clean off his face.

And my heart could leap at the sight if it had wings.

"You're joking." He smiled again, nervously. "Say you're kidding."

"You know I don't joke about business, honey." I winked. "You taught me that."

"To *who*?" he asked, snapping his laptop shut. "Who the *hell* did you sell it to?"

"Private equity firm," I answered. "Terms are clean. Non-negotiable. They'll fold in the rest of the expansion plans and keep my name on the brand."

"You... you *can't* do this *without* the board."

"Oh, Julian, I already have," I said smoothly. "The board agrees. With my share, I didn't *need* a consensus. I just *needed* a decision. *Mine*."

"Ari," he exhaled. "Come on. What about the brand?"

I smiled.

"The brand will be fine, Julian." I gestured toward him. "You were *always* better at selling a dream than building. So, sell, honey."

He snatched the folder off his desk, flipping through its pages in a panic.

Didn't take long before his back straightened, eyes shooting up at me.

"You gave *that bartender* rights to our bar's fucking menu?! Are you mad? Have you gone insane?"

His breath left in a loud gust, eyes wide, voice sharp.

"Ari," he said again, like my name could still hold weight. "We *built* that menu. *We* paid for that. You and I. How could you just... *give* it to *him*?"

"*His* ideas," I said with a cool shrug. "*His* name. *His* legacy. *Yours* was always borrowed."

"Shit," Karmen whispered to my right.

"So, you just... just..." He let out a scoffing laugh. "Plan to build this *boy* up or something?"

"Or something," I said, turning on my heels and walking toward the door.

"Wait!" Julian shot up behind me. I could see his reflection in the glass ahead of me—stunned, small.

"Ari, please, let's just... slow down a second. Maybe I crossed a line, I'll admit that. But you and me?" He stepped closer, fingers brushing mine, his tone dropping to a whisper. "I never stopped loving you. You know that, right, baby?"

I focused Karmen's way to see her straining her ear to hear us.

I moved my eyes on Julian again and he stepped closer.

"Let's just *think* about this right now."

"Thought about it," I said, sliding my hand free from his. "And decided, as you can see. And so we're clear? This love you still have for me? Not mutual. So be a good man for once and lie in the bed you made, *baby*."

I turned for his glass door, opening it. "Everything you need is in the folder, Julian."

I shifted my attention to Karmen, looked her up and down, taking in all the money Julian siphoned from me to build her shiny little life only for him to be in my face telling me he still loved me. After all that. Pathetic. Hated that for her.

I blinked the sight away. Not my problem. Never was.

"You think you're free of me, Ari?" he asked.

"I've *been* free, Julian," I told him, not even bothering to turn back again. "You were just the last person to realize it."

"Julian?!" Karmen snapped, walking up beside him at the door. "What does this mean?"

"It *means* don't worry, girl," I said, pressing the elevator's call button. The doors opened immediately, and I stepped on. "I'm leaving the empire intact. You can *still* play empress... just in a *much* smaller castle."

I used my hands to show her, fingers an inch apart.

"Much, much smaller. Damn near tiny, Karmen. Enjoy, love."

Before either of them could get another word in, the elevator doors closed between us.

In that moment, I didn't feel rage for once, or regret. Just relief. I hadn't burned a bridge and I'd kept my hands clean... just like my mother and her quiet power. All I'd done was removed the leash tethering me to them.

I could've done this a while ago. But fuck it... I was doing it now. I was ready. And I had something — or someone — to look forward to, far from here. Or at least I hoped.

I dipped my hand into my bag on the ride down, pulling out the sticky note Charmaine had given me. I smiled.

It was only an address, but for some reason, I felt a pull in my chest reading it. It was like Micah was speaking to me across an entire ocean.

I figured if I showed up at Le Cordon Bleu, I might run into him—at least that was the plan before Charmaine gave me this sticky note.

The air felt easier to breathe the moment I stepped out onto the lobby floor.

The city outside, louder, brighter, more beautiful than ever.

I slid into the black car I'd been riding in all day, leaned back against the seat, and exhaled everything in my lungs like I'd just walked out of someone else's skin.

Because I did.

The last of my mask was gone.

My name, still mine.

My freedom, finally real.

Next stop: Paris.

And hopefully, Micah would be welcoming to my arrival.

Day 42: Lose Your Fear

MICAH

The morning was still on my Juliet balcony.

The sun had just risen, painting the cobblestone streets below in *grillz* gold. A few early risers moved about, their footsteps soft and scattered.

I lifted my mug, lips brushing the chipped ceramic as I took a sip of coffee.

Picked it up at a little friperie near my flat my first week here —just needed something to get by. Kept it even after I bought better ones. Guess I got attached.

Summer was beautiful out here. Paris was beautiful.

I was in Paris.

A Black kid from Crown Heights Brooklyn now living in a spot with a clear view of the Eiffel Tower between buildings.

It was exactly what I imagined... except lonelier.

I breathed in the scent of warm bread wafting up from the café downstairs. Every time I stepped onto this balcony, it felt like the city exhaled with me.

My flat sat on the third floor, close enough to the street that I could hear the clatter of morning life. And still, it was peaceful. Quiet in a way Brooklyn never was.

I drained the last sip of coffee and stepped back inside.

Bare feet padding across parquet floors, I passed the exposed brick wall and paused briefly at the small memorial I'd created— my father's urn, a few framed photos of him and my mom, candles I lit every evening, and his watch he gave me when I turned twenty-one. I had taken it off when he died, returning it to him by keeping it beside his memorial.

After my dad passed, Brooklyn felt heavy with ghosts. Every corner was a memory. Paris wasn't an escape... it was a beginning I'd been quietly dreaming of for years. And for the first time in a long time, I wanted a beginning more than I feared an ending.

My new place felt like home, which was wild considering I hadn't even been here a full month. But I'd made good on what I told myself—I'd spend whatever it took to feel grounded in this new country, and I did.

Paris was everything.

Soft breezes. Storybook streets. Early morning silence.

But by night... my thoughts wandered.

They wandered to *her*.

I sat down on my couch and leaned my head back, letting my thoughts drift like they had been all week. No class today. No grocery run. No prep. Just time. Too much of it.

I'd resorted to Googling her some nights, just to see her face again.

Arielle.

Every photo of her had this poised elegance, but I couldn't stop noticing the sadness behind her eyes.

She looked her happiest when she forgot who she was supposed to be.

That night... in her home... in her bed... being herself.

With me.

I wondered if she still thought about me the way I thought about her.

A few weeks after I landed, I'd called her office. Gave her assistant my new address in Paris.

I knew it was risky. Definitely suspect.

The ex-bartender giving the boss a foreign address? Yeah. I knew what it looked like.

But I had to leave something behind. A breadcrumb.

Proof that I still thought about her. That I was still thinking about her every day and I was here if she ever wanted to follow the trail.

Some days I felt like a little boy, crushing hard as hell on a grown ass woman. Other days, it felt like something more. Bigger. Realer. Meant to be.

I sighed heavily, stood and headed for the kitchen to tackle the breakfast dishes.... when there was a knock at the door.

I paused, hand still midair.

Nobody knocked here. I didn't know anyone yet. Not like *that*.

I crossed the living room slowly. Peered through the peephole.

And froze.

Arielle.

She was standing on the other side of the door.

My heart kicked so hard I thought it might break through my ribs.

"The fuck," I whispered.

I blinked, hard. Felt like I was seeing things. Then I unlocked the door and pulled it open without even thinking.

She stood there in a yellow sundress that hugged every curve like it knew them intimately. Expensive high heeled sandals that sparkled on her feet. One hand resting on her designer luggage. A soft, cautious smile on her lips.

No designer pantsuit clinging to her shape, no serious yet elegant expression on her face. Even her hair was different. Not straight, but curly, and framed her face in a way that made her look softer. Lighter. She looked like she belonged in a gallery, instead of a boardroom.

She stood there... not as the woman everyone relied on at *The St. James*, but as the woman finally letting herself be.

For me?

"So," she started, "You quit working for me, for *this*, huh?"

I was at a loss for words, my mouth trying hard to form a word, a sentence, something, but failing me.

"It's softer than I expected," she added. "Your flat? Very Parisian."

I released a breathy laugh.

"Hi, Micah," she whispered.

My breath caught in my chest. My cool, gone. Completely gone.

I couldn't even speak. She was *here*. I was just thinking about her—*wishing*—and now *here* she was.

The fastest manifestation of my life. I hardly ever got what I wanted... until now. And damn, she was even more than I'd let myself imagine.

She laughed under her breath, still smiling. That same smile I fell for.

"So..." she started again, her eyes flicking past me, then back to mine. "Are you going to invite me in, or...?"

Her voice was so soft. A little unsure.

She looked like everything I remembered and more than I deserved.

But she was here—yellow dress, soft smile, beautiful bouncy curls, and no fear in her eyes.

And I wasn't about to waste another second.

I stepped forward, slid my hand to the side of her face, and gently cradled her jaw in my palm.

Her hand pressed flat against my bare chest as I leaned in and kissed her.

Really kissed her.

I wrapped my arm around her waist and pulled her into my

orbit. Slid my hand past her jaw and into her hair, anchoring her to me.

Her kiss was soft at first, then desperate, urgent in the way that said she missed me just as much as I missed her.

I kissed her like I'd thought about her every day. Because I had.

I'd imagined this moment a hundred different ways.

None of them came close to this.

When we finally broke for air, I pressed my forehead against hers, chest heaving.

"You're here," I whispered, eyes closing.

She nodded, hands gently resting on either side of my neck.

"And this time..." she said, her voice steady and soft, "I'm not running."

I smiled and wrapped my arms tighter around her. Not out of shock or relief... but peace.

Real peace.

"Good," I remarked, leaning in to kiss her again. "Because I'm not letting you go this time."

She laughed, a quiet sound that filled the entire flat.

"I believe you."

I stretched one arm behind her, grabbing the telescopic handle of her luggage, then took her hand and led her inside.

Arielle stepped out of her sandals and let her eyes roam the flat, soaking in every detail.

Her gaze landed on the memorial shelf.

That's where she walked to first.

She paused there, in front of it, glancing over at me.

"Your parents," she said softly.

"My parents," I echoed.

She nodded, tracing her finger gently along the edge of my father's urn.

"You've got your mom's eyes and your dad's smile. They were beautiful."

"They were," I said quietly.

"They would've been proud of you," she whispered, looking around again. "This place... it's perfect. In here and out. I forgot how stunning Paris could be."

I bit down on my bottom lip, dragging my teeth over it without thinking.

"Well..." I said, watching her walk toward me, "I hope you get to stay long enough to see how beautiful it can be... with me."

Arielle slipped her arms around my neck, her smile soft and knowing. "Have I ever told you how sexy I find it when you do that thing with your lip?"

I smirked and shook my head.

"Well, since I'm here indefinitely..." She grinned. "I'll have plenty of time to show you exactly what it does to me."

A sigh slipped from my lips before I even realized I was holding it in.

"I spent so long trying to be what everyone needed," she confessed. "And I never asked what *I* needed."

She kissed my chest once, then rested her head there.

"It's this." She nodded, looking up at me again. "It's *you*, Micah. I need the *original*, right?"

"Right." I nodded. "And you deserve. *We* deserve."

I wrapped my arms around her waist again, and we just stood there.

Still.

Breathing each other in.

Then she leaned forward, closing the last inch between us, and our lips met with a sigh we both couldn't hold back.

One kiss. Then another... slower, deeper, lips parting like neither of us wanted to stop.

She whispered against my mouth, "Show me our room."

That was all I needed to hear.

I lifted her easily, her legs winding around my waist, her arms draped over my shoulders like they'd always belonged there. She smiled when I bit down on my bottom lip, and the sound she made in return—low, throaty, unguarded—lit something in me I'd never forget.

I carried her down the hall, not rushing, not desperate. Just sure.

Because there was no what-comes-next waiting at the threshold.

There was only us.

Two people who finally stopped trying to fix everything around them, and instead... finally chose to just be.

Epilogue – Lose Your Clock

Eighteen Days Later...

ARIELLE

I darted across the street, pausing just as a Vespa zipped by, its breeze lifting the hem of my lavender tea dress. I clutched the rolled-up fashion magazine tighter to my chest to free a hand as I reached for the café door.

Before I could even step onto the welcome mat, I heard, "Arielle!"

The way Collette, the café's owner, said my name—with that lilting French accent—warmed me in ways I never could have expected.

"*Oh mon Dieu, je dois te dire.*" She rushed up to me, eyes sparkling. "You are a genius!"

I laughed. "*Bonjour*, Collette."

"*Bonjour*!" she beamed. "*Tu vas pas croire ce qui s'est passé—*"

"Oh God, whoa! Collette, Collette." I held up a hand, already grinning. "English, please. I only know *bonjour*, remember?"

She hollered a laugh that made me love her more.

Paris.

I was living in Paris—and I loved every single moment of it.

It had only been a few weeks, but I had already claimed this café as *mine*. Since my second morning here, I'd come every day. And Collette? She'd become one of the best parts of those days.

"Your idea," she said, taking my hand and guiding me to the counter, "to leave the... *uh*... the samples?"

I nodded. "*Mmm-hmm.*"

"Yes, to leave them by the register," she continued excitedly. "So that people could taste and want to buy? It worked. And the points card system you suggested?"

"You started using the rewards card?"

"*Oui*! And I punched the first one to give them incentive to come back. It's brilliant! Over five people returned today with their card in hand."

"It's not *brilliant*, I promise." I smiled. "Just an age-old suggestion. *You* made the perfect macaroons *and* the amazing coffee. *You're* the genius"

She waved me off, disappearing behind the counter. "You're too beautifully stunning to be this modest."

I laughed.

Laugh lines were starting to form around my mouth, and for once in my life, I didn't care. I'd been laughing more in the last month than I had in the last twenty-five years. Even my brothers noticed.

"Is she laughing more, Miles, or am I hearing things?" *Langston asked.*

"Definitely laughing more," Miles replied. "And I know why."
I smiled to myself listening to them.

"So... the bartender, huh?" Miles added.

"Personally," Langston chimed in, "I was shocked."
They'd called me at the end of day four in Paris.

They were the only ones I wasn't ignoring. Yet. I was starting to wonder if I'd have to add them to that block list too.

"All right, let's hear it," I said, draping my arm over the iron balcony railing. The Eiffel Tower sparkled between buildings.

"What do you two have to say about it? I mean... I don't really care but I am curious."

Micah had just finished cooking dinner. I was full, ready for bed, but couldn't ignore my brothers' call.

"I'm proud of you," Miles said first.

I jerked my head back.

"Same," Langston added. "In fact, I can't wait to meet the guy who got Arielle St. James to abandon post and go AWOL. He must be something special."

"Ha. Ha," I replied with zero expression.

"Dad said twenty-eight?" Miles asked.

"I don't think it's bad," Langston jumped in. "Dad's dating a thirty-something-year-old."

I groaned. "Please, don't remind me."

"If everyone else can do it," Langston continued, "big sister should have a little fun, too."

"It's not like that, you two," I said, peeking behind me. Micah was settling onto the couch, catching my eye and blowing a kiss that made my stomach flip.

"Ohhh, it's not like that," Miles teased, dragging it out.

"It's not," I insisted, turning back to the view. "Micah has his own aspirations. His own dreams. His own money."

"We're not talking about that, Ari." Langston chuckled. "You know damn well what we're talking about."

I giggled while shaking my head. "It's not about that either, guys."

"Oh, so are you two saving it for your second marriage or something?" Miles teased. "Sleeping in separate beds to maintain chastity?"

"Please." Langston snorted. "I'm pretty sure that young man is putting her through that Parisian mattress every night."

I gasped. "Oh hell no."

They both howled with laughter.

"I will end this call right now! You know me." I shook my head.

"You two are sounding like a couple of Park Avenue gossip girls at brunch."

"I can't wait to meet him," Miles said, still chuckling. "I'll let you know when I'm in Paris next."

"Same here," Langston added. "Might make it one of my future sabbatical stops."

I rolled my eyes. "Sabbatical."

"Yes, sabbatical," Langston said smoothly. "Welcome to the world of loving everyone from a distance."

"Uh-huh," I mumbled. "And until the money runs out and you can't afford your next sabbatical?"

"Oh no, big sis," Miles said. "We love and watch from a distance... but when things get too crazy, we step in. It's a beautiful balance. You're gonna love it on this side of bliss."

And they weren't wrong.

Because I did so far.

I really, *really* did.

"Today's coffee is on the house," Collette insisted, returning with my order.

I shook my head. "Nope. You listen to my ideas if you want, but I still pay for *my* coffee."

She groaned dramatically, and I laughed—loud and full, the kind that comes from somewhere deep.

Collette had no idea who I was. Most people in Le Marais didn't... and I loved that just as much as I *loved* the place itself.

Crooked charm, cobblestone streets, bistro tables spilling onto sidewalks like Collette's. The light here was golden. The air? Sugared with espresso and croissants. It was a dream. And I was living it—finally—with a man who felt like the finishing touch.

I had no clue what was happening in New York. Just knew the wire transfers landed when they were supposed to. I wasn't fighting for cooperation or to be heard. I was just *being*—and being had never felt this good.

"Here you go," Collette said, handing me my drink. "I still say it's free."

"And *I* still say nope. Here." I handed her my card.

She giggled, accepting it.

I glanced around her charming café, now alive with movement, patrons chatting at tiny tables, the smell of something sweet in the air. When I'd first walked in weeks ago, Collette was slumped behind the counter, chin in hand, bored out of her mind.

Now? She was serving.

My father said a lot of things when I told him I was leaving the business, but he was right about one: I *was* business to the bone. Couldn't help it. When making money is your ministry and you do it for decades, it becomes a part of you, for better or for worse. I walked into her shop and saw a hundred ways to grow it. Felt the itch to give it that *Midas touch* my dad always spoke about.

But I hadn't opened a single finance report from *The St. James* since I'd arrived in Paris.

And I didn't miss them. Not one bit.

Still, old habits die hard.

Sliding my credit card back into my wallet, I sighed and gestured toward the front.

"Put your specials on a chalkboard outside," I told her. "Half your business is just walking by and wondering. Let them know what you're serving. Use language they can *taste*. Don't say *'chocolate croissants available inside.'* Say *'fresh-baked chocolate croissants. Still warm. Flaky layers. Melting chocolate.'* Make them taste it before they *taste it*. Then reel them in with... *'Gone by noon. Taste before the clock catches you.'"* I winked.

Her face lit up like sunrise.

I sipped my coffee—decadent, rich—and sighed. If she kept making coffee like this, I'd keep giving her every bit of strategy I had.

"No discounts, no freebies for me," I told her with a smile. "Just... coffee. And if it's good, I'll say so. You go from there."

"*Merci beaucoup!*" she squealed. "*Mon Dieu... tu es un vrai génie!*"

I had *no idea* what she said—but I would, with time.

"Okay," I said, placing my cup down. "Tomorrow, I want to order in French. So walk me through it again. I want to say *more milk, just a little sugar.*" I motioned with my hands. "Teach me. Nice and slow this time."

MICAH

French jazz floated in from the open windows, curling through the air like smoke. It mingled with the smell of flour, butter, and the faint scent of espresso from the café downstairs.

I stood barefoot over the counter, dusted in flour, joggers slung low on my hips, my black tee powdered white. I was prepping a tart I'd learned in class last week, a promise to Arielle. And she promised to help. Said she wanted to try. I was still waiting to see that with my own eyes.

Arielle St. James baking? Yeah, I had to see that.

I glanced at the altar near the brick wall. My dad's urn sat there with a photo of him and my mom, his old watch beside them like a time capsule. I talked to them often... sometimes out loud, sometimes just in my head.

The grief was quieter now. Still there, but softer. A pain with rounded edges.

Then I felt her.

Before I saw her, I *felt* her.

Arielle padded across the parquet floors barefoot, curls piled high, beautiful brown body draped in that forest-green silk slip that had *my* body betraying me before I could blink. The one that clung to her hips like it was made for her. The view made my focus slip.

She walked right up behind me and leaned her head against my back.

I exhaled, the moan automatic. Her warmth against me made it hard to concentrate.

She'd disappeared for a few hours earlier. Long enough for me to miss her. But she came back, like she always did.

Paris made her soft. Curious. Free. She made friends with shop owners. Dished out business advice in her own quiet, brilliant way. She was still a boss, even when she tried not to be.

A few weeks back, I noticed deposits hitting my account. Not small ones, either. Many of the deposits were in the thousands, daily. I thought maybe it was something from back home, related to my father's life insurance. Until one night over wine and cheese, I mentioned it, and she told me they were from my time at *Vesper.*

"You wanna run that back?" I asked, eyes fixed on her.

She sipped, shrugged. "I said the deposits are for the drinks you created at Vesper," she repeated. "The patrons still order them. And every time they do... you get a portion of what they pay."

I stared at her like she was magic.

"And, Micah, they order them a lot," she added, grinning. "As you can see from over 3,000 miles away."

I have no idea how she did it—and she's never gone into detail —but I don't need her to. She says she's not "business" anymore, but it's in her marrow. The difference now? It's not *all* she is. And I love that.

Arielle kissed my back as I stirred the lemon filling. Her fingers traced around my chest, light and teasing, making it damn near impossible to focus.

If I made it through this tart without tossing her ass on the floured counter, it would be a miracle.

Her hand slid down to the waistband of my joggers, fingertips dipping inside, tracing slow circles through the fine hairs, making me hard.

I bit my lip, feeling the pull to touch her win over whatever self-control I thought I had.

"You're distracting the chef." I smirked. "Very rude."

"Oh, then I'm about to get disrespectful," she whispered.

I chuckled. "Didn't you promise to help?"

"Did I?"

I took her hand from my joggers, spun her gently in front of me, making her laugh.

"Come here," I said. "Let's roll the dough."

She washed her hands and joined me. I guided her through it, placing my hand over hers, moving the rolling pin with her.

That question I asked her that night at *The St. James Table*—after the kitchen had closed and we found ourselves alone—came back to me... *"You ever think about just... letting it happen?"*

I was watching the answer unfold in real time.

She was softer now. Open. Flirty. A never-ending turn-on I wanted to protect with everything I had.

"Not too much pressure," I whispered, leaning in behind her. She shivered and I smiled. "Let the dough guide you."

She glanced over her shoulder. I brushed flour off her cheek with my thumb, close enough to kiss her, but I didn't. Not yet.

I'd imagined her here in Paris with me. But never like this. Not this peaceful. Not this perfect. With her actually here, in real life... it felt like I was living out a dream.

While the tart baked in the oven, Arielle and I stretched out on the couch. Her head on my bicep, her leg draped over mine, our lips brushing, tongues teasing, hands wandering.

She couldn't keep her hands to herself, which meant I had to keep mine out of the way. For now.

She liked having her way with me. And I liked watching her indulge at my expense. Every time, without fail.

Her fingers traced my chest, then up to my face, gently turning it so she could kiss me again.

I never knew what time it was when I was with her. Didn't care unless I had to be in class. When it was Arielle and me—it was just Arielle *and* me. And I made it a point to get lost in us.

Her soft hands slipped under my waistband, teasing my dick through the joggers, her eyes locked on mine. No words. Just the heat between us. Just wanting. Both of us knowing we'd give in soon enough.

After a long pause, she giggled.

"What?" I asked.

Her grip eased off my stiffness, her hand trailing up my chest before she shook her head, smiling at me. "I was just thinking earlier in the shower... about when I was twelve, and all the girls at school were *oohing* and *ahhing* over the cute boys... and I just didn't get it. I didn't see what they liked about them. I honestly thought something was wrong with *me* for not being interested. Thought I'd *never* meet the guy that would make me *oooh* and *ahhh*."

Her smile curved slow, mischief sparkling in her eyes. "Turns out... the one who could really make me *oooh* and *ahhh* just hadn't been born yet."

I snorted, laughter spilling out. I dug my fingers lightly into her stomach, tickling her. She squirmed, laughing uncontrollably until she stilled again, her eyes back on mine... clear, full of something *deep*.

"I love you, Micah," she whispered, her voice trembling, the words so raw they gripped me. "Is it too soon to say that?"

I brushed my thumb across her forehead, holding her gaze. "Too soon?" I shook my head. "If it is, fuck it. I love you too, Ari. More than I can say."

I still couldn't believe how much my life had changed in such a short time... and yet it felt like I had been waiting my whole life for a moment like this. For a woman like *her*.

"And to think..." I licked my lips, grinning. "All this happened because I cut you off in traffic."

She laughed, wide and real. "No. This all happened because

you're the most amazing man I've ever met. And, Micah, that's saying a lot—because I've met plenty of men in my world. But none of them even come close to you."

I folded my bottom lip into my mouth and bit it.

She moaned, climbing closer, crashing her lips to mine. "You have no idea how sexy you are when you do that."

And just like *that*, our soft kisses became something else.

Tongues, hands, need. Everything between us igniting.

The timer dinged in the kitchen. Our tart was done.

Neither of us moved.

We just kissed deeper, breathed harder, and let ourselves get lost again.

I pushed her slip dress above her hips and slid the seat of her panties to the side to ease into her nice and slowly.

"*Mmm*, wait," she sighed, eyes fluttering shut. "You have to get the tart out of the oven."

I kissed her throat, hips pressing deeper, my voice low against her skin. "Forget the tart... I already got somethin' sweeter right here."

"*Mmm-hmm*," she moaned. "So *much* sweeter. *Oooh*, right there."

I groaned. "Right *here*?"

She giggled, the sound breaking into another moan before she lifted her head and crashed her lips into mine.

This was what *losing track of time* really meant.

Because I never expected love. Never planned for it. Didn't see it coming.

But Arielle taught me something I'll hold forever...

Love doesn't follow your timelines. It creates them.

THE END.

Author's Note

Thank you for reading *How to Lose Control in 42 Days*.

This story lived in my ideas folder for years. I always wanted to write something centered around a luxury Black hospitality brand, but it wasn't until rewatching *Soul Food* that Arielle St. James truly came to life. If you've followed this story's journey on my socials, you already know: Teri Joseph inspired Arielle. It's why this book is dedicated to her.

I always felt Teri deserved more. But rewatching the film at my big age, I went from believing she deserved more to wanting to create that more for her. I never saw the spinoff, so I don't know if Teri ever got her happy ending. To the movie's credit, *Soul Food* wasn't a Black romance film, but I view life through a romance lens. Can't help it. I'm always searching for the love, even in the smallest frame. And I felt Teri deserved real love.

We don't choose our families. Sometimes they feel like home; other times they make us feel like outsiders. With this story, I wanted to show that no matter how complicated love or family can be, choosing yourself is always an option... the most important one. You can't pour from an empty cup.

Micah was sent to fill Arielle's cup, and in many ways, she

filled his, too. This was my first time deeply exploring an age-gap romance, and these two stretched me as a writer in the best ways.

If this is your first read by me, welcome to my world! You've got some catching up to do. If you've been here from a book (or many) ago, my heart is so full. Thank you for trusting my pen, for loving my characters, and even for fussing at them when they frustrate you. We're stepping into a beautiful new era, and I can't wait for you to see what's next.

Wherever you joined me from, thank you. Your support means everything.

See you at the end of the next book.

With love,

BK

Are You New Here?

If you're new to my work—or just want to dive deeper into the stories that fill my catalog—you'll love having my Character and Book Connections Guide in your possession.

The guide breaks down all of my stories by tropes and reading vibe, helping you find your next favorite based on what you're in the mood for.

You'll also find a character connections section that maps out every main character, where their journey began, and where else you can find them across my interconnected book world.

The guide is updated periodically, and when you add the PDF to your BookFunnel library, you can refresh anytime to download the latest version.

So if you're not ready to leave my book world just yet—and want to discover which story matches your current vibe—click the link below to download your free copy.

Copy + paste the web address in parentheses into your browser to download BK's Character & Book Connections Guide!
(https://dl.bookfunnel.com/4ke5nuffu6)

About the Author

Brookelyn Mosley is a captivating voice in the world of black romance literature. With a gift for weaving heartfelt narratives and steamy encounters, she invites readers on journeys of love, passion, and self-discovery. Through her compelling storytelling, Brookelyn celebrates the beauty of black love and explores the complexities of relationships with authenticity and depth. With over 50+ titles, her stories resonate with true-blue readers, touching hearts and inspiring conversations about love, identity, and resilience.

Connect With Me Online!

Facebook: http://facebook.com/brookelynmosley
Facebook Reading Group: Brookelynites Book Lounge
Instagram: @Brookelynmosley
My Website: BrookelynMosley.com
My Readers Website: BKBookLounge.com
My Mailing List: https://brookelynmosley.com/bk-insiders-club/

www.ingramcontent.com/pod-product-compliance
Lightning Source LLC
Chambersburg PA
CBHW031411310726
48971CB00003B/821